KILLERS CAN'T HIDE

A NOVEL

A DELBERT CANTRELL MURDER MYSTERY

TRAVIS SHORT

Publish Authority

Killers Can't Hide
ISBN 978-1-954000-68-1 (Paperback)
ISBN 978-1-954000-69-8 (eBook)

Editor: Janie Mills
Cover Design: Raeghan Rebstock

Published 2023 by Publish Authority,
300 Colonial Center Parkway, Suite 100
Roswell, GA USA
PublishAuthority.com

Printed in the United States of America

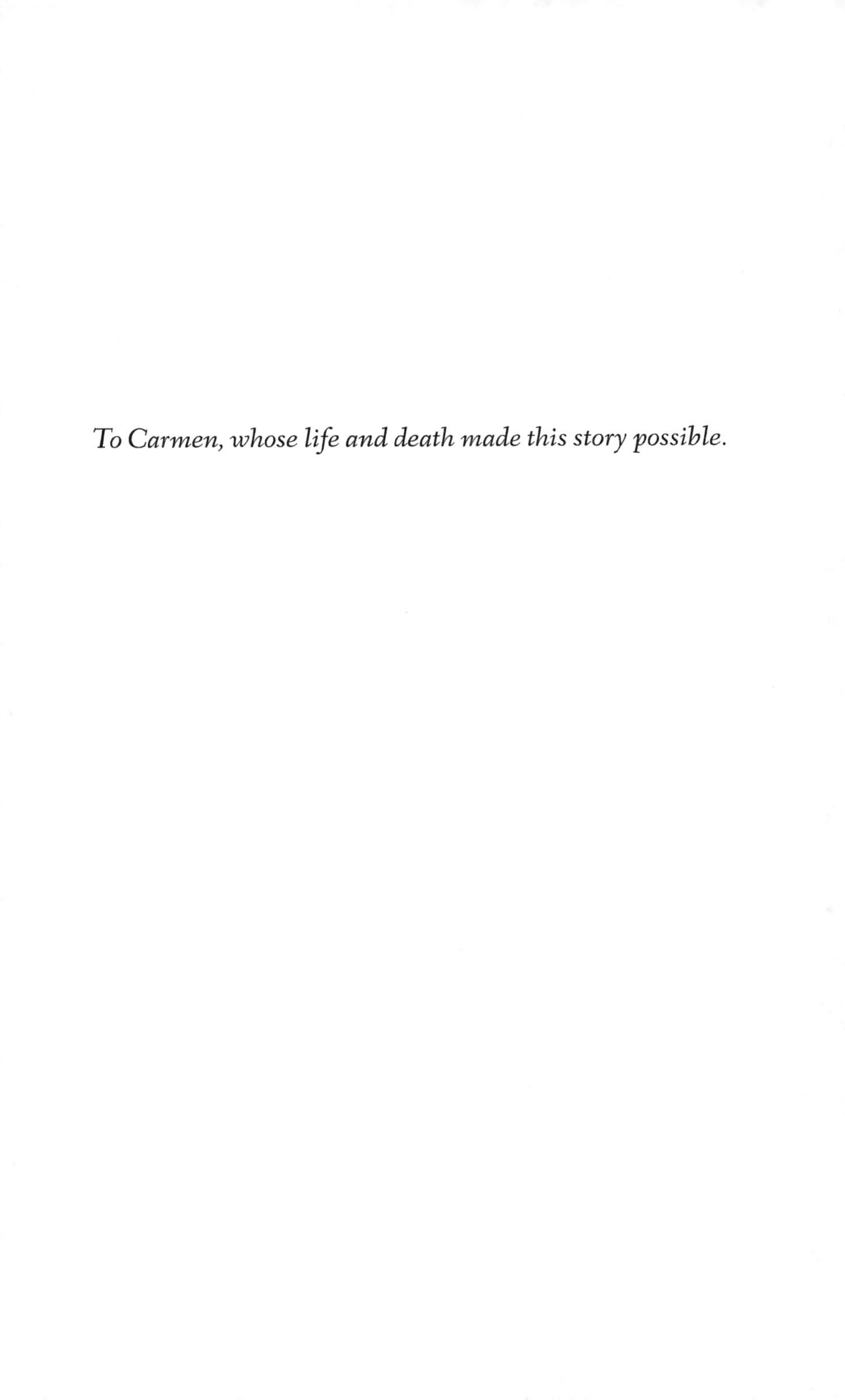

To Carmen, whose life and death made this story possible.

The course of love never did run smooth.

— WILLIAM SHAKESPEARE

1

NUMBER ONE SUSPECT

I don't know if I was awakened by the blue lights sweeping across my upstairs bedroom window or the rapping of the deputy's nightstick against my front door—one or the other brought me out of the first decent sleep I had had in weeks. I sat up quickly on the side of the bed and slid a foot into one of my shoes while simultaneously reaching for the old gray robe I had thrown across the foot of my bed a couple of hours earlier. I shoved my second foot into the other shoe as I sidled toward the bedroom door leading to the stairway.

"Just a minute," I yelled, loud enough to awaken whoever is buried in Grant's tomb. "I'm coming; I'm coming, for God's sake." Wiping the sleep from my eyes with the sleeve of my robe, I approached the door at the foot of the stairs.

Deputy Harlan Hanes, all five feet, six inches of him, was poised to strike another deafening blow against the door about the time I opened it. He looked as if he had been bitten by a snake when I opened the door and said, "What the hell is going on, Harlan? Why in the hell are you beating down my goddamn door this time of morning?"

And while he stammered to answer, I continued, "Why the hell you driving that goddamn piece-of-shit patrol car onto my lawn?"

"Sorry, Delbert," he finally said, "but I come out here to tell you that Carmen is ..."

"What?" I asked impatiently. "Fucking some other bowlegged piece-of-shit drugstore cowboy?"

"No, Delbert," he said, almost swallowing his words. "She's dead."

"No, shit," I said, grinning. "You fucking with me, Harlan?"

"No, by God, I ain't, Delbert. Honest to God, she's dead, dead as a doornail."

My knees went a little weak. I leaned against the doorframe and gathered my thoughts. "Who in the hell...," I muttered aloud, then thought, *Somebody finally killed her rotten little ass.*

I backed into the hallway and motioned for the deputy to follow me. He closed the door behind him and continued to talk as we both sat down on the living room sofa.

"We don't know, but for sure, you're goin' to be the number one suspect, Delbert. After all, she still is your wife —even if you are separated."

"Who said that, any damn way? Doesn't matter. I wouldn't have killed her. I damn well should have, but I wouldn't't."

"Sheriff wanted me to let you know what's bein' said, so you can get your story straight."

"Well, Harlan, go back and tell John he's got nothing to worry about with me. I was here all night, and in my bed for the past two or three hours."

"That won't be good enough, Delbert. She was killed sometime in the evenin', long before midnight. Sheriff said you need to come down to the funeral home to identify her."

"Shit fire! You mean John can't identify Carmen Cantrell?"

Harlan just looked at me with a dumb ass grin on his face. I couldn't help but think I was watching Barney Fyfe in action, but as I recalled, Barney was much taller than Harlan.

"Loudermilk must be the only son of a bitch in this county that doesn't know her from topside down or bottom side up." I patted my robe pocket as I looked around the living room for the keys to my pickup truck.

"Goddamn, Delbert, the woman's dead. Ain't you got no respect at all? Not even for the dead?"

"Guess not, Harlan, but I would think this bullshit could wait until tomorrow morning.""

"Jesus! Suppose they make me testify 'bout how you acted when I told you she was dead." His eyes were only halfway visible under the brim of his cap. "It ain't gonna look pretty—and I gotta tell the truth."

"When did the truth become such a precious commodity to you, Harlan?"

"Goddamn! I am an officer of the law."

"And a damn good one too."

"Thanks," Harlan said, obviously not understanding my subtle derision.

"Don't forget to tell them how broken up I was, Harlan. Tell them how I cried."

"Christ, Delbert, she's your wife—or used to be your wife."

"That little gold-digging bitch? She wasn't my wife—she was just married to me. You know the difference, Harlan?" Then I thought to myself: *No, you poor dumb bastard. Judging from that fat ass broad you're married to, you couldn't possibly know what I am talking about.*

I got up from the sofa and went upstairs to change into street clothes, mumbling every curse word in my vocabulary. I heard the crackling of Harlan's radio but couldn't make out his exchange with the dispatcher back at the sheriff's office. After dressing, I bounded down the stairs, pushed open the door, and motioned to the deputy. "Let's get this show on the road. I want this shit over with as soon as possible."

"Yeah, let 'er rip, I say." Harlan giggled and preceded me out the door. I got into my truck and waited for him to crank up the patrol car. Just before he closed the driver's side door, he yelled back at me, "Follow me, Delbert."

Christ, I thought, *He's going to make a goddamn spectacle out of both of us.*

I called him every kind of son of a bitch in the book as he sped away, digging up six feet of my carefully manicured lawn. Blue lights flashed, and the siren wailed as we burned rubber down the two hundred feet of my paved driveway and onto the main county road. I was glad it was pitch dark outside and that no one could see me following Harlan at eighty-five miles an hour. At each intersection, he set off the siren and pushed his patrol car into the passing gear. I was right on top of his ass, just the way I was sure he wanted me to be. It was Harlan's big night, and I knew he wanted to make enough noise to alert the local news reporters of our arrival at the county courthouse in Maysville. What I didn't know was that when I stepped down from my truck, that little weasel, Harlan, would try to slap a pair of handcuffs on me.

I pushed him away and attempted to get back into my truck. "You dumb fucker, Harlan; you can't arrest me without some kind of evidence."

Two more deputies appeared out of the dark and wrestled me to the ground.

Harlan stood triumphantly above me. "We got the evidence, big shot, and we're goin' to hang your ass this time."

I knew he was talking about the run-ins I had experienced before with the sheriff and his band of illiterate deputies.

Harlan stood tall, talking in the direction of the television cameras, and proudly announced, "Delbert Cantrell, I am placing you under arrest for the murder of your wife, Carmen Cantrell."

Not more than a minute later, Sheriff Loudermilk pulled up in front of the courthouse and got out. Leaving the door (the one with the two–foot gold and black star painted on it) open, he double-timed it, his beer belly preceding him, to where I was standing. Facing the camera, he lauded Harlan for capturing the suspect of the generation single-handedly.

"Got anything to say, Mr. Cantrell?" He spoke more to the camera than to me.

"Yeah. Have you ever heard of something called an arrest warrant?" I made an attempt to kick Harlan in the balls but almost fell on my back. "You train this stupid son of a bitch, and where's my fucking lawyer?"

"Scrub that! Scrub that!" the sheriff yelled in the direction of the TV camera. At six-foot-three, his ten-gallon hat made him tower above me., "Goddamn, Delbert, you can't say that on television ... Jesus, have a little goddamn respect."

The TV cameras were still rolling.

"Look, John," I said over the top of the rumblings and hoots and hollers from the crowd that had been attracted by all the patrol car lights and sirens. "If you are trying to get reelected, you may have just been outdone by your deputy."

"What the hell you talking about, Delbert? That smartass mouth is sho'nuff goin' to get you in some real trouble one of these days."

"I mean, Harlan is the hero here, isn't he?"

The sheriff held up his hand to block the camera. "Just you remember wiseass, Harlan and every other swingin' dick on this force works for me. One way or another, I am in charge of every operation, includin' arrestin' killers who commit crimes in my county. I had your ass arrested, Delbert, and I'm goin' to make sure you get what you deserve."

"I want to see your warrant."

He held up a piece of paper and waved it a couple of times before stuffing it into his vest pocket. "I got it right here, bigshot, and your money ain't goin' to save your ass this time."

He shoved me in the direction of another deputy, making certain there was no more gratuitous publicity for Harlan.

"Book this sumbitch and stick his ass in a holdin' cell 'til tomorrow mornin'."

"I want to call my attorney."

"We'll make sure you get to call him in the mornin'." His pigface grin reminded me of Napoleon from the novel *Animal Farm.*

I shook loose from the deputy and ran head down in Loudermilk's direction, striking him mid-belly. My hands were behind my back as I held the fat bastard on the pavement with my body. He squirmed beneath me. I chomped down on his left ear. I held on until a nightstick from somewhere came crashing against the side of my head.

It was 10 a.m. the next morning, Saturday, when I woke up in a steel cage in the basement of the courthouse.

2

BOLOGNA FOR BREAKFAST

When I regained my senses that Saturday morning, it took a few minutes for me to comprehend my surroundings. Looking around, I saw three other steel cages, all empty. *Christ, guess I'm the only criminal in the county.*

In the farthest corner, I made out the soles of someone's boots as he sat with his feet on the desk, reading what appeared to be a paperback novel. I yelled across the room. "Hey, asshole. What am I in here for?"

The officer stood. I could see it was a tall, lanky deputy by the name of Elrod Jones, the only decent son of a bitch in the sheriff's department. I laughed out loud. Elrod and I were once pretty good drinking buddies until both of us ended up divorced, and I won fifty million in the Florida lottery and married Carmen. "Damn, Elrod, you get all the tough assignments—guarding the number one criminal in the state of Mississippi."

He got up and sauntered toward my cage, a wry smile

crossing his rough-hewn face. "Take it easy, Delbert. I'm not goin' to make it hard on you."

I moved to the front of the cage and stuck my nose through one of the four by eight openings. "What all they got me charged with?"

Elrod came to the cage and casually took hold of one of the flat bars running up the front of the cell. "Oh, nothin' much, 'cept murder, resistin' arrest, and assaultin' a police officer, namely one fat ass by the name of John Loudermilk—nothin' to worry about, Delbert." He was grinning like a Cheshire cat, obviously enjoying the moment much more than I was. I halfway expected to see him disappear, leaving nothing but his pointy-toed boots and wiseass grin.

That was pure Elrod—one of the good ole boys. He could always make you feel all right, even under the most dire circumstances. I might have gotten a real kick out of his sense of humor if he was the one in the cage and I was looking in at him. I suppressed an urge to laugh and replanted a serious scowl on my face.

"I want my goddamn lawyer."

I figured you might. Already called Sydney Saperstein's office this morning, first thing. Got a message he won't be in 'til Monday. Guess you'll be my guest 'til then. How's your checkers game?"

"There won't be any checkers with me. I'm getting the hell out of here."

"Like I said, Delbert, you're gonna be my guest for the weekend 'cause ain't no way of gettin' you out of here 'til you see a judge and post bail."

"You know damn well I didn't kill anybody, let alone Carmen Cantrell."

"Fuck, Del, John Loudermilk knows that too, but he wanted to get his damn face on TV. You know we got an election comin' up, and John is in trouble."

"That son of a bitch hasn't seen trouble until he fucks with me."

"Just cool your heels, Delbert, and let Saperstein take care of things Monday. Murder may not be your problem, but resistin' arrest and assaultin' may cost you a couple of bucks."

"That may be so, Elrod, but that bastard better watch his ass when I get out of here. He's had it in for me ever since I won that lottery, and now I got it in for him."

"Like I said, just cool your heels for a couple of days. Won't be too bad. Meantime, you want some breakfast?"

"I don't want any damn breakfast. I just want the hell out of this dog cage."

"Better have some breakfast—fried bologna and gravy. Biscuits ain't bad. Long time 'til supper."

"And what's for supper, Elrod? Caviar?"

"Bologna sandwich." He bent over laughing and came up with tears in his eyes.

"Elrod, you know what you can do with that bologna? Shove it right up your ass sideways with both hands."

"Delbert, tell you what. This afternoon, the sheriff is goin' to take you to the funeral home to identify Carmen."

"You mean they got me locked up and don't even know if it is really Carmen?"

"Oh, they know all right. Next of kin has to identify her, just a formality, and maybe just a little bit of humiliation for you and another chance for the sheriff to get on the evening news. All part of the process. But what I was goin' to say was that I would get you a cheeseburger or a pizza while you were in the sheriff's custody and have it waitin' here when they bring you back."

"You know what you can do for me? Let me out of this cage so I can take a piss and wash this blood off my face and hands."

"OK," he said, "but I'm s'posed to handcuff and shackle you before I let you go to the bathroom. You ain't goin' to pull no shit, are you, Delbert?"

"Course not, Elrod. I don't want you on Loudermilk's shit list too."

He unlocked the cage and walked with me down a hallway to the men's room.

"You want to come in and hold my pecker for me?" I grinned broadly before shutting the door behind me.

I washed away the blood from a two-inch gash over my left eye. Two bulbs were burned out in the overhead fluorescent, so I couldn't see much in the cracked mirror, but was able to make out a goose egg-sized bump above my left ear. I mumbled a few choice curse words before taking Harlan Haynes's name in vain. "One of these days, Harlan, I will kick your dumb ass above your shoulders." The sudden thought that his ass was already above his shoulders made me laugh again.

Elrod cracked open the door. "You all right in there, Delbert?"

I came out zipping my fly. "I'm fine. Just had a thought about Harlan Haynes being elected sheriff. That's enough to make you laugh or cry, one or the other, maybe both. Just think, Elrod, he might be your boss soon."

"That's when I'll be coming to you for a job, my man."

"Hell, no. You're too damn tainted, worked too long for John Loudermilk. Besides, I may be doing time for murder or sitting twiddling my thumbs on death row."

I think that got to Elrod a little bit. He placed his hand on my shoulder. "Come on, Delbert. I ain't kicked your ass in a good checkers game in at least five years."

I would have felt a whole lot better if he had just laughed it off.

It was close to 1 p.m. when I heard the sheriff and his deputies talking to Elrod. I must have been sleeping, worn out after being subjected to Elrod's prowess on the checkerboard. I sat up, rubbed my eyes, then stood to get a look at John Loudermilk's fat ass as he bent over the deputy's desk. He looked back and pointed in the direction of my cage. "I'm goin' up to my office. Get Delbert ready, handcuffed, and shackled. We'll take him out of here in about ten minutes."

"No need to shackle him, Sheriff," Elrod insisted.

"Ahright, Jones, but if he gives me any shit, someone may bust his head again, and I'm goin' to hold you responsible for the whole damn mess." Loudermilk made sure he spoke loud enough for me to hear.

I held my hands through the window in the cage door while Elrod handcuffed me. As he opened the door and motioned for me to come through, he spoke calmly, barely above a whisper. "Don't give these assholes any shit, Delbert. They'd love to have an excuse to kick your ass. It would get them in good with our beloved sheriff."

Deputies Stu McCarty, a pock-faced thirty-year-old who had never held a job before getting on Loudermilk's goon squad, took hold of my left arm and ushered me toward the door. Deputy Logan Vice, whose last name was more than appropriate, followed behind, holding his nightstick in his hand, occasionally slapping it across his palm, a little reminder that people of Cumbersome County had nothing to fear with these two on the job.

By the time I was settled in the back seat, I made up my mind to be a perfect citizen on the ride to and from the funeral home. I half expected McCarty and Vice, both of whom I had shared a beer during my drinking days, to lean on me, but they were too busy impressing each other with their tales of sexual opportunity and conquest.

Vice described a lady he pulled over for speeding the night before. "Good lookin', maybe forty."

"Yeah?" McCarty obviously wanted details.

"Blonde?"

"Yeah."

"Real blonde?" McCarty chuckled.

"Didn't get a chance to find out, but I got a invite. Her old man is goin' out of town for three days next week. Two kids'll be in school all day. Hot damn. I may just be patrollin' her neighborhood." Vice slapped his leg and laughed, braying like a nutless mule.

McCarty had obviously developed a sudden admiration for his fellow officer. I was only guessing that with his pockmarked face, he didn't get the same invites that the six-foot, brawny Vice was privy to. And so McCarty wanted more. "What happened? I mean, how'd you get it all set up?"

"Well, Stu, it was like this. She was probably doin' forty

in a thirty-five-mile zone. I started to not pull her over, but when I got a look at her, man, I just decided to give her a shot. Turned on the blues, hit the siren. Two minutes later, I had her name and address, and she was lookin' up at me through those long lashes. 'You aren't goin' to give me a ticket, are you, Officer?'"

McCarty squirmed in the driver's seat. I thought he might start masturbating. Instead, he fished for more titillating details. "What'd you say, Logan? What'd you say?"

"I said, 'Ma'am, I sure don't want to.'"

"Then she said, 'I'll do anything.'"

"And you know, Stu, when they tell you that, you better make sure you're armed with condoms."

McCarty broke out laughing, stopped, and then sat up taller in his seat. "I ever tell you about the time..."

I was sick of the BS "You better watch the goddamn road, McCarty. Take it you haven't had too much pussy in your life, at least none you can really brag about."

He shot back. "Hey, old man, bet you can't even get it up anymore. May be why that beauty queen wife of yours left you. 'Sides, I've had my share of pussy. I guarontee."

"Maybe," I said, "But looks like Mr. Vice done got a whole lot more than you."

"Shut the fuck up, Cantrell. Your money don't cut no shit with me. You give me some more shit, and I'll stop this car and bash your goddamn skull."

It sounded to me as if he meant it, so I shut up.

WE ARRIVED AT SALVATION FUNERAL HOME A FEW minutes ahead of the sheriff. As we waited, Stu McCarty flipped through his ticket book while Logan Vice looked into the mirror, combed his hair, and preened. The only thing I could think about was how much I would like to catch one of these young bastards alone, without a gun and badge. *Hell, let him keep his gun. I will just shove it up his ass.*

Our tranquility was broken by the roar of the sheriff's engine as he screeched to a stop alongside our patrol car. He got out and motioned for his deputies to follow him into the funeral home.

We were met inside by the coroner, Benny Pruitt, and the funeral director, a short, pudgy little twerp, dripping with insincerity, by the name of Palmer Lovett. I was sure he would appreciate having the desirable body of Carmen Cantrell in his custody. Rumors abounded that Palmer paid special attention to his female cadavers.

Pruitt led us through double doors into a back room filled with caskets. We passed through another door into a smaller room, no more than fifty degrees in temperature. A body lay on a gurney, covered with a white sheet. We gathered around. Pruitt pulled back the sheet and folded it across her breasts. Carmen lay motionless, appearing as if she was sleeping. "That's Carmen." My voice was emotionless, but I couldn't help thinking how wickedly beautiful she was, even in death.

Pruitt pulled the sheet back up, covering her face and long blonde hair.

I looked at the sheriff and then at the coroner. "That's it?"

"Yes." Sheriff Loudermilk was emphatic.

I turned to the coroner. "What's your verdict?"

Coroner Pruitt eyed Loudermilk. "She's dead." Both men smiled at the verdict.

Only my handcuffs prevented me from reaching across Carmen's body and strangling Pruitt. "How did she die, you son of a bitch?"

Deputy Vice took hold of my arm. "Come on. Delbert. Let's go before you get yourself in more trouble."

"I'll go willingly when I get an answer from the coroner. I want to know how she died."

The sheriff shot back. "Thought you could tell us that, Delbert."

"Fuck you, Loudermilk."

Deputy Vice pushed me toward the door, away from the scowling sheriff.

I yelled back toward the coroner. "Send her body to Hattiesburg for an autopsy. You people are too fucking dumb to find the cause."

The sheriff roared at me. "You ain't callin' the shots here, Delbert. I am."

"You can discuss it with Sydney Saperstein on Monday, Sheriff." Those were my last words before I was led through the doors and shoved into the back seat of the patrol car.

Vice and McCarty got in, and we sped away.

McCarty turned to me. "Delbert, you ain't got good sense, but I'll be damned if you ain't got balls."

3

DISCOVERING PETE PITCHFORK

On the ride back to the courthouse, the deputies opened up. They appeared to have developed a little admiration for my standing up to the sheriff. I assumed it was because they didn't have the guts to do it themselves. But when your job is on the line, you see things differently, just as McCarty and Vice probably did. The difference was that I had nothing to lose by telling John Loudermilk where the bear shits in the woods, especially since there were at least five witnesses, six if you include Carmen. Knowing her, though, she might have enjoyed seeing the sheriff cram a nightstick up my ass. She would believe I deserved it.

Deputy Vice stopped looking at himself in the mirror and turned to talk to me through the metal screen that separated us. "How much do you know about Sheriff Loudermilk, Delbert?"

"Well, guys, I know he's a prick. He's been throwing his weight around for a long time. I've known John Loudermilk a lot of years, even before he became a deputy, and that had to be at least twenty years ago. He was a prick then. He's a bigger prick now."

That brought a chuckle from Stu McCarty. "I ain't sayin' he's a prick, but I'm not goin' to argue with you either, Delbert. After all, he approves my paycheck every two weeks." He chuckled again as if what he had just said was clever as hell.

Logan Vice chimed in. "Well, what I was gettin' at .... You probably know the sheriff is one vindictive son of a bitch, and when he thinks someone done him wrong or embarrassed him, he finds a way to get even. I'd watch my shit a little better if I was you, Delbert."

"I appreciate that advice, boys. I really do."

McCarty looked straight ahead, avoiding my eyes in his rearview mirror, skepticism in his voice. "You didn't kill her, did you, Delbert?"

"Course he did," Deputy Vice answered for me, sounding as if I should be proud of what I was accused of doing. "I know damn well if she was my wife and she was cheatin' on me, she would damn right be a dead woman, just like she is."

"Well, she's dead all right, but I didn't do it. It hurts to admit, but I still cared about her."

Vice spoke up again, "Enough to split half what you own with her?"

I thought I should explain a few things to the two dumbasses in the front seat, "I could never have killed her over money even though I can be a selfish bastard. Like I said before, I guess I still cared too much about her. And, boys, I hope you know Mississippi is not a community property state. I was rich before I married her, and she didn't have a pot to piss in. Besides, I already spent a half million on that ranch of hers. Loudermilk better come up with another motive if that's his thinking."

The deputies were silent for a moment, I guess sizing me up a little more.

I leaned forward, making sure both deputies heard me. "You boys trying to get a confession out of me? Sheriff didn't put you up to that, did he?"

McCarty spoke up. "No, Delbert, for sure. Just that seein' you stand up to the sheriff gave me a different outlook —kinda made me respect you."

Vice piped up. "Hell, I would have more respect for you if you did kill her. From what I hear, she liked to spread her stuff around."

"You can't believe everything you hear, Logan." Two nights earlier, I would have punched his lights out for running off at the mouth even if what he said were true. Instead, I scooted back in my seat and crossed my arms. As far as I was concerned, our conversation was over. I gathered that Stu McCarty was almost convinced of my innocence, but Deputy Vice wasn't too sure. It would just have to stay that way for the time being.

For the next fifteen minutes, I didn't say anything. Just closed my eyes and attempted to shut out the road noise and palaver from the front seat. It took only a few minutes for McCarty to revive the conversation about Logan Vice's impending conquest. "When are you goin' to see that gal? The one you stopped for speedin'?"

"Probably Tuesday." Without opening my eyes, I knew Vice had a shit-eating grin on his face.

"Think she's got a friend?" There was a plea in McCarty's voice. It was then I decided how hard up the boy was, even though he was married, and made myself a promise to buy him a piece of ass when I got free.

"I don't know, but hell, you can have her after I get through. I ain't lookin' for no long-term relationship."

McCarty scoffed, "Hell, I don't want your sloppy seconds." Then he swallowed a guffaw.

"No, I mean, I'll introduce you if she's willin'."

Their intellectual conversation ended when the car came to a stop in back of the courthouse, and Logan opened the car door. "We're home, Delbert."

Elrod Jones was standing by his desk. It was obvious he had been alerted by radio to expect us.

"He's all yours, Elrod." Logan Vice let go of my arm. "Be seein' you, Delbert. Hope things go OK."

I played to his ego. "Thanks, man. You too. Hope she's a real blonde."

He looked back and gave me a thumbs-up as he exited. "I'll let you know."

And I thought: *You miserable little fuck. I hope her husband comes home early and parts your hair down the middle with that Glock 22 you carry.*

Elrod must have read my mind. "What an egotistical asshole! Thinks he's God's gift to women."

"I gathered that," I said. "Heard anything from anybody?"

"Yeah, as matter of fact, Saperstein called. Checked his messages and got back to me."

"What'd he say?"

"He wanted to know what in the hell was going on. Said the sheriff didn't know a damned thing about the law he had sworn to uphold. He muttered something about a dumb bastard."

In all my dealings with Sydney Saperstein, I had never heard him curse or even raise his voice. He was always cool as a cucumber, always cautioning me to watch my temper, especially when we were in court. From what Elrod was telling me, I assumed Sydney was as pissed off as I was. Just that I had a bashed in scull, and he didn't; that gave me a little more reason than Syd to curse.

"Next thing he said was for you to not get your head cracked for mouthing off. Of course, I told him it was already too late for that."

"Bet he got a kick out of that."

"Yeah, he chuckled, but only after I told him you had survived."

"He says for you to put a cork in it and wait for him to get back. He's in Birmingham but going to cut short his visit and come home tomorrow afternoon. He'll be here first thing Monday morning to bail your ass out. To be precise, I think he said *your dumb ass.*".

"I pay him a bunch just so he will heap that kind of praise on me."

"Worth every penny." Elrod removed my handcuffs. "Need to take a piss and wash your hands before we eat? Got you a pepperoni pizza in my desk."

"Beer, too?"

"How about a Coke?"

"That'll do if it has to."

"I got to put you back in your cage before our illustrious sheriff comes in."

I went down the hall to the restroom. Elrod lingered close by, but didn't follow me. When I returned, he opened the cage door and locked it behind me. "Oh, yeah," He said, "You made the morning news on all three channels and in the *Pascagoula Town Crier and Mobile Crimson Times*. After lunch, I'll let you read all about yourself."

"No, let me look now."

MILLIONAIRE CHARGED WITH WIFE'S MURDER. That was the headline in the *Town Crier*. Underneath was a photo of Sheriff Loudermilk holding onto my arm. I appeared dazed. I assumed the photo was taken after I got the nightstick across the side of my head. But it could be that killers are just supposed to look dazed after they've been captured. Deputy Haynes was visible in the right edge of the picture, poking his head into view of the camera. I kept thinking how glad I was that Harlan got a little publicity. After all, he had worked harder than the sheriff to capture this dangerous killer. Besides, it would really piss off Sheriff Loudermilk, seeing that Harlan got into the picture too.

I unfolded the other newspaper to see what they were saying about me in the neighboring state of Alabama. Fortunately, bigger news had taken top billing because on the same day Carmen's body was discovered, the governor of Alabama was forced to resign because of sexual misconduct. A much smaller headline, halfway down the page, declared: MISSISSIPPI MILLIONAIRE MURDERER—

Prominent Cumbersome County Resident Charged with Killing Wife.

It's one thing to hear about someone being falsely charged with a serious crime. It's a whole different matter when you are the one being charged. I had the sobering thought that we were not playing games and that I might get railroaded for something I didn't do. I couldn't help but wonder why Sheriff Loudermilk was so eager to pin the whole damn thing on me. I knew I would be out of the pokey once Sydney Saperstein got back into town, but I would still have Carmen's murder hanging over me while her killer walked around free.

Elrod's booming voice broke the silence as he came toward my cage, a Coke in hand. "Want some pizza and Coke?"

"Just lost my appetite." I held up the folded newspapers.

"Come on," he said. "They got nothin' to hold you on. Loudermilk was grabbin' at straws on the chance you choked Carmen to death. He was hopin' you might just up and confess."

"It'll be a cold day in hell when I confess to something I didn't do. And Elrod, you know me, and you know I'll get that fat bastard when this shit is all over."

"Don't tell me that, Delbert. It could land both of us in trouble."

"I'm sorry, buddy. Sure don't want to take you down."

I had almost forgotten what a good friend Elrod was. He had always been by my side in every barroom brawl I got into. He was tougher than hell—honest, too. There was no way he would ever perjure himself on a witness stand. I knew then it was time for me to shut up and listen.

"How about some pizza, Delbert?"

"Yeah, think I will."

He pulled a chair up by my cage, and we ate our pizza without talking. When I finished my third piece, I asked, "How much do I owe you, pal?"

"Delbert, now you're goin' to piss me off, and you won't have anybody lookin' out for you in here."

"Same old Elrod. Don't let anybody pay for anything."

"You know my sayin', Delbert, 'don't take anything off anybody and don't take anything from them.'"

"I remember," I said, "and I'm sure glad you were on today. By the way, who comes on when you get off this evening?"

"Marge Wilson. You remember her, Delbert. She's been with the sheriff's department for almost four years now."

"She one of Loudermilk's girls?"

"Hell, no. Her husband is twice your size and meaner than a pissed-off cobra. She's a good gal. I'll scoop her in before I leave."

I lay back on the cot and kicked off my shoes. "Got anything to read besides these fucking newspapers?"

"Yeah, matter of fact I do. I just finished reading a crime novel, kind of a Mike Hammer spoof, *My Gun Cries Justice.*" He laughed. "Hero's name is Pete Pitchfork."

"Any good?"

"Aah, it's okay, not too long. But there's a crooked-ass police chief in the story that might remind you of a mutual acquaintance of ours. Oh, and there is a blonde beauty in the story who might sound familiar."

Elrod walked over to his desk and returned with a paperback novel. He tossed it through the opening in the door. On the cover was a front-on shadowy picture of a man wearing a black raincoat and fedora hat. In his right hand was a .44 Remington Magnum aimed directly at the reader.

I opened the book and began the first chapter, "Murder on Main Street."

4

TOO BEAUTIFUL FOR HER OWN GOOD

Halfway through Chapter 1 of *My Gun Cries Justice*, I began to see similarities between our sheriff and Police Chief Thomas Toolbox. Even though the book was written as a spoof of Mickey Spillane's Mike Hammer, the author captured the characteristics of the real-life John Loudermilk. In fact, I could envision our sheriff pushing his way through the door of Pete Pitchfork's office and announcing, "Mr. Pitchfork, you are under arrest for the murder of Carmen Cantrell." I was hooked and didn't lay down the book until I finished the fourth chapter.

About 6 p.m., Marge Wilson showed up, ready to take over the guard duties from Elrod. Except for the uniform, she could have passed for my sister—matronly looking woman, few years older than me, big smile with a deep south dialect. For a few minutes, she and Elrod stood by the desk talking, occasionally looking in my direction as if I was a long-tailed orangutan at the zoo. I got off the cot and stuck my face into the opening of my cage door.

"Can I get in on this conversation, guys? Or maybe I could swing by my tail."

Elrod didn't look my way but showed me his middle finger. They went on talking in hushed tones.

Marge moved closer and introduced herself. Her voice reminded me of Carmen, throaty and sweet as sugar. "Honey, you just take it easy. I'm going to treat you right while you're under my care. Elrod told me what a raw deal you're getting from the sheriff and his wanna-be."

"Yeah," I said. "One is a damn jerk, and the other an out-and-out prick."

She laughed heartily. "Don't have to guess which is which."

"She's all right," I said to Elrod. "You're leaving me in good hands. You coming in tomorrow?"

"Yeah, I'll be takin' you off Marge's hands at six in the morning."

"Before you go, can I get something to eat around here?"

"Are you ready for a bologna sandwich? That's all we got, and the bread's stale."

Margie spoke up. "Don't worry, Mr. Cantrell..."

"Please, Marge, under these circumstances, Delbert will sound real good. It's better than anything I'll hear from the sheriff."

"Ok. But, as I was saying, I've got plenty in my brown sack. Got some good meatloaf left over from supper. Ralph liked it a lot." She chuckled. "But Ralph likes anything."

I assumed Ralph was her husband. "Thanks, Marge. I'll make it up to you—maybe take you and Ralph to dinner when I get out of here."

By then, Elrod was heading for the door. He looked back

and mouthed off one more time, a wide grin on his face. "Don't go anyplace, Delbert. See you at six."

I wished like hell he could take my situation more seriously. He was having way too much fun at my expense. But that was the kind of relationship we had during our drinking days. I might have given him the middle finger too, but he never looked back.

AFTER ELROD LEFT, MARGE MADE A MEATLOAF sandwich and handed it through the opening in the door. I thanked her. She said nothing, just nodded, then walked down the hallway. A minute later, I heard quarters dropping into the Coke machine. She came back and handed the can to me.

"I owe you one, Marge."

"Fifty cents won't break me. We get 'em a little cheaper here in the sheriff's department. But I'm sure he would like to charge more. It would let him skim the profits the machine takes in."

"The way I hear it, he's got his hooks into everything already. I'd really like to know how many people he's protecting or shaking down."

Her eyes grew wide as if she was eager to tell someone something she had held back a long time. "Well, you know that big house he's building out on the point? He sure can't afford that on his sheriff's salary."

"No wonder Harlan Haynes wants to be sheriff!"

"God forbid. But then, I don't guess it could get much worse."

I began eating. Marge went to her desk. After a few moments, she turned on the television hanging on the wall. A local news reporter was rehashing the Carmen Cantrell murder, the biggest news event for Cumbersome County since Bob Dole made a campaign stop at the county fair in October 1996. My ears perked up, and I stopped eating while I squinted to get a side glimpse of the image on the television. I recognized the voice of Charlie Chambers, a local reporter from Biloxi, as he brought the public *up to the minute* on the case. "Delbert Cantrell, estranged husband of the victim, is being held in Cumbersome County lockup. He will face a preliminary hearing before Magistrate Jerry Parson Monday morning. According to a spokesman for the sheriff's department, there are no other persons of interest."

Marge turned down the volume so I wouldn't hear any more.

"It's OK, Marge. All right here in the paper." I yelled across the room and held up a copy of the *Pascagoula Town Crier*."

She got up and walked toward me. "Does the paper say how she was killed?"

"No, just that she was found yesterday morning in the tack room of her barn. She runs quarter horses, you know. She has six or seven of her own and boards about twenty more for other people. So, could have been anybody."

"Why'd they arrest you?"

"The estranged husband always does it, doesn't he? Sure as hell wasn't brilliant detective work, I'll tell you that. Six weeks before election, and I hear tell the sheriff is trailing his deputy in the latest poll. Harlan grabbed me thinking he could get one up on his boss."

"I don't think it worked, do you? The sheriff got most of the publicity."

"Yeah, he heard Harlan was bringing me in and got to the courthouse in time to hog the television coverage."

"I'm surprised the sheriff had the guts to arrest you."

"I don't think Harlan left him much choice. Once the sheriff learned his deputy had me following him to the courthouse, he had to act as if it was his idea. He may think twice about that decision when my lawyer finishes with him. Sydney Saperstein may teach John Loudermilk something about the law."

She shook her head, apparently disagreeing with my assessment. "Around here, he is the law. He's one of the good ole boys, and he knows the judges will back him up."

I took the last bite of my sandwich. "Marge, do you mind letting me out of here to go to the latrine?"

She opened the cage door.

"You gonna put handcuffs on me?"

"No use for that," she said. "You aren't going to go anyplace. Besides, if you try, I'll just have to shoot you."

I hoped she was kidding, but there was no smile on her face. Right then, I sized her up as tough as nails—sweet as pie, but tough as nails. I bet Ralph didn't give her much grief.

When I came back, she locked the cage door behind me. "You know, I met your wife a few times when she was selling real estate. I think her name was Carmen Tucker back then, married to Gary Tucker."

I sat down on my cot. "That's right. She was married to Tucker at one time." I chuckled. "But he was long gone when I met her. By then, she had stolen another gal's husband. His name was John Williams. I stole her from Williams. I didn't know what the hell I was getting into."

"I thought she was really nice."

"She was nice—a great gal in many ways and had a lot of friends. Of course, we had our differences, but she didn't deserve what happened to her. She loved those damned horses and that ranch. That's why I bought it for her."

"I went out there once."

"Where?"

"Oakwood Ranch. Matter of fact, Harlan Haynes and I went there. I guess a couple of cowboys got into a squabble and ended up coming to blows. We broke it up and sent them on their way without any charges. Never did learn why it all started."

"I could make a pretty good guess, I'll bet. It wouldn't have been the first time a couple of studs came to blows over Carmen Cantrell. She had that kind of an effect on men. She was too beautiful for her own good."

"Do you have any idea who might have wanted her dead?"

"No. I don't think anyone wanted to kill her. Oh, maybe some jealous wife might have thought about it, but the way I see it, this was done in a fit of passion."

"Do you know how she was killed?"

"I don't know. That excuse we have for a coroner thinks she was strangled. I've demanded an autopsy. My attorney will take that up with the judge on Monday. I'm going to make sure they have one hell of a time pinning her death on me. Not only that, I want to get my hands on the son of a bitch who did it."

"I hope you do, Delbert. You don't deserve this."

"I just might start by confronting those two cowboys who were fighting at the ranch. I know a few of the boarders. Word gets around in a hurry, and someone out there at Oakwood knows what was going on."

She moved away from my cage, but after a moment, turned my way. "I heard the sheriff recently bought two horses. You might want to find out where he got them."

"Hmm, wonder where he keeps them."

I opened up my paperback to Chapter 5 and began reading.

5

———

WAITING FOR SAPERSTEIN

The lights were out at 10 p.m. except for a couple of nightlights showing the way down the hallway toward the restrooms and the light on Marge's desk. I lay staring into the semidarkness, having just completed Chapter 5 of *My Gun Cries Justice*. By the end of that chapter, I developed admiration for the fictitious sleuth, Pete Pitchfork, not because he was brilliant, but because of his tenacity and determination to stand up to a corrupt police chief. Although there were no apparent similarities between the gunning down of a pernicious police captain and the murder of Carmen Cantrell, the author had coincidentally embodied the cunning traits of John Loudermilk, sheriff of Cumbersome County, Mississippi in the author's chief of police, Thomas Toolbox. And I could understand that, in spite of Pitchfork's outward bravado, he must have experienced the kind of uneasiness I was feeling as an innocent man accused of murder. And, like Pitchfork, I would never show that side of me.

I tried running through a list of names of men who were known or rumored to have kept company with Carmen. Some I viewed with incredulity, wondering how in the hell she could have associated with them under any circumstances. However, it's probable some folks held similar opinions of Carmen's and my relationship. But there was the little matter of fifty million dollars that made me mighty attractive to her and many other women who might not otherwise have wasted two minutes of their time on me. Since Carmen and I separated, my reputation as a player held me at a safe distance from serious romantic entanglements. But it didn't work that way with her. She drew men to her like flies to honey, especially married men, tired of their dumpy little wives who, unlike Carmen, no longer resembled the high school sweethearts they courted and married. And she always fell madly in love with them for a little while, at least until the next one came along. I supposed one of her cowboy Lotharios wouldn't leave when it was his time to go. The way I figured it, that would be her killer.

I turned onto my side, attempting to find a comfortable position on the canvas army cot that served as my bed. After several uncomfortable minutes, I changed sides, fluffed my half-size pillow, and closed my eyes. Less than an hour later, I was awakened by a light going on, the clanging of the adjacent cell door, and the mutterings of my new, inebriated neighbor.

I sat up and looked around me, startled for a moment, before understanding a Saturday night reveler had been arrested, most likely for driving under the influence. After a few seconds, that assumption was confirmed.

The prisoner fumbled through his pockets, apparently as confused as I was after having had my head bashed in by Harlan Haynes. "Whasa fuck am I doin' in the slammer?" He managed to utter those almost intelligible words in Marge's direction, his tongue pushing drool through his lips onto the leather vest he wore over a decorative red-and-black western shirt.

Seemingly unruffled, Marge continued back to her desk, sat down, and began to write in her log.

The inmate walked three steps to the corner of his cage closest to Marge. "Hey, lady, I said whasa fuck am I doin' here."

Without looking in his direction, she responded. "Drunk driving, and, oh, yes, a suspended license. You're not going anyplace for a while. So shut up and go to sleep. You might make more sense when you're sober." She turned out the light.

The man grabbed two vertical bars on the side of the cage and attempted to shake it. "Fuck you, lady, thas what I say. Fuck you."

I called to Marge. "Let me get in there with him, and I'll flatten his ass, Marge. I might like to kick some drugstore cowboy's ass anyway."

She stood. "Can't let you do that, Delbert, as much as I would like to." She raised her voice to make certain he heard. "One more outburst, Gerald, and I will have you transported to the adult detention center for lockup."

He shut up and sat down. I lay back on my cot, wondering who my neighbor might be. I turned to watch as he sat, removing his boots and tossing them into the corner of his cell. *Gerald, Gerald, I know that man.* "Are you Gerald Hinson?"

"Who the hell are you?"

"Never mind," I said. "I thought I might know you, but I guess not." I would wait until morning for a better look.

BETWEEN THE SNORING OF MY DRUNK NEIGHBOR AND my inability to get comfortable on the army cot, I managed to catch two hours of sleep before the lights in the cell room came on at 6 a.m. Elrod was already sitting at the desk where I had last seen Marge sometime early in the morning before I fell asleep. When he saw that I was standing, he came to my cage. "Morning, sleeping beauty, want some coffee? Just made a fresh pot."

"Yeah, black if you don't mind. How long you been on this morning?"

"Twenty minutes, maybe half an hour."

"Why so early?"

He went across the room and came back with a mug of coffee. "I couldn't sleep, and I thought Marge could use a break. So, I came in a few minutes early. Louise was on the rag last night, chewing on my ass about money." He reached the cup through the bars. "She's a good gal, but damn, I wish she'd get off my ass. I'm doin' the best I can. She ought to know that."

"You know what I think, Elrod? Women are a pain in the ass—even the best ones."

"Not Louise, not really. She's usually real supportive.

Things get to her once in a while, and she can't help but let me know about it."

"You ever consider leaving this damn job?"

"Sure," he said, "plenty of times, but what the hell can I do? I'm not like you, Delbert. I don't have a college degree and my own company. Hell, I barely finished high school."

"Well, I got mighty lucky. I did okay before winning that lottery. But it set me up for life. Don't have to work another day if I don't want to. No more driving a dozer or running a crew of retards. I just do it to keep busy. That's a pretty damn good feeling."

"I wouldn't know." He walked back toward his desk. Maybe I heard a little resentment in my friend's voice.

I called after him. "You ought to come to work with me."

He didn't turn to look at me. "Don't want no charity. Delbert."

"No charity, Elrod. I don't give money away." My next thought made me chuckle. "Except to Carmen maybe. I bought that goddamn ranch and it's done nothing but cost me money ever since. No charity, Elrod. I could use a good man like you."

"I would say this is not the time or place to discuss something like that."

"Does that mean you're interested?"

"Maybe." He sat down at his desk. I couldn't tell whether he was pissed or just tired of talking.

"OK. I'll be out of here tomorrow. We can talk about it then."

Elrod didn't respond. He was a proud man, and he wanted no favors from me or anyone else. I hadn't given him much thought in the past couple of years. But the jail episode got me thinking how much help he could be. I needed someone I could really trust, especially while I was fighting for my freedom and perhaps my life. Elrod Jones could be my lifeline. He just needed a little time to come to that realization.

The basement floor of the courthouse, where our cells were located, was quiet as a cemetery except for an occasional grunt from the adjacent cell. Elrod must have grown tired of the grunts because after an hour or so, he got up from his desk and walked in our direction, a metal cup in his hand. He raked the cup across the side of the cell, the loud rattle causing me to sit up straight. "Piss call, Hinson. On your feet."

The man sat up. "What the fuck?"

"On your feet, Hinson. This ain't no spa."

Hinson retrieved his boots from the corner and began slipping them on, grumbling all the while, finally saying something intelligible. "Where am I goin'?"

"Take a piss and wash your face. I got breakfast coming from the detention center."

"Bet it's a goddamn banquet."

"You'll love it, cowboy, shit on a shingle, except this is shit on a biscuit. It may be cold by the time it gets here, but it will still make a turd."

Hinson grumbled some more, wiped the cobwebs from his scraggly beard, then stood. Elrod opened the cage door and pointed the man down the hall in the direction of the restrooms.

After he had disappeared through the door, I asked, "That Gerald Hinson?"

"Yeah, you know him?"

"Not really, but I know about him. I think he spent a couple of weeks at the ranch, supposedly working for Carmen. Now that I laid eyes on him, I can see he's a real catch. No wonder he lasted only two or three weeks."

"Partner, I can tell you he is a real fuckup. He's been arrested a dozen times, at least three for drunk drivin'. That's why his license is suspended."

"Aren't you concerned he might try to take off on you?"

"He ain't got the guts, Delbert. He knows I'd kick his ass if he tried to get out of here. And he knows I'm right here waitin' for him."

On cue, the bathroom door opened, and Hinson sauntered back to his cage, got in, and waited for Elrod to lock him up again.

"You wanna go wash up, Delbert?"

"Yeah, and I gotta piss like a racehorse."

BREAKFAST CAME ABOUT EIGHT, SERVED IN A Styrofoam container. The creamed chipped beef was cold and pasty. After a few bites, I called to Hinson, "You want my breakfast?"

"Yeah."

We both reached our arms through the bars and he took the container, "Enjoy," I said with a malicious grin.

He began to eat his second helping. "What they got you in here for, man?"

"Murder."

"Who'd you kill?"

"No one, yet. But I might before I'm through." I raised myself by the cell bars to appear taller than my six feet and more ominous than I was.

"You Cantrell?"

"Yeah, I'm Cantrell, and I think I've heard of you."

"I hope nothin' bad."

"No, all good." My temperature was rising, and I needed an excuse to get out of my cell. I yelled toward Elrod. "Another head call, buddy."

When I came out of the bathroom, Elrod motioned for me to sit in a chair by his desk. He handed a broom to me. "Hold onto this in case the sheriff or one of his boys decide to pay a Sunday morning visit. That way, I can say I had you sweeping down."

"What do you want?"

"To talk."

"Talk?"

"Yeah, you got something better to do while we're waiting for Saperstein to bail your ass out?"

6

SAPERSTEIN TAKES CHARGE

Spending Sunday in a dog cage in the Cumbersome County courthouse basement was not what I had planned when I went to bed the previous Friday night. Then, I was blissfully unaware that my estranged wife, Carmen, was lying stone-cold dead on a stainless steel table at the Salvation Funeral Home. And I was totally oblivious to the possibility that an empty-headed deputy would be smashing my door down at 2 a.m. with that news. Now I sat, listening to the pissing and moaning of my fellow inmate and hoping like hell the creamed chipped beef he had eaten that morning contained an unhealthy dose of strychnine.

By noon, in spite of the unpleasant noises coming from the adjacent cage, I finished reading *My Gun Cries Justice* and settled back on my cot, rehashing the story in my mind while waiting for the day to pass. About 12:30, lunch arrived from the detention center. This time, the bologna sandwiches had cheese on them, which made them almost edible even though the bread was at least a week old. I was grateful to Elrod for the Coke he got from the machine in the hall to help wash the sandwiches down. After that gourmet meal, I could hardly wait for the gastronomical treat I was sure would be offered for dinner. It was no wonder people like Hinson kept getting themselves locked up. Where else but jail could you experience such exquisite cuisine?

My hopes for Hinson's demise were dashed when I heard sputtering and coughing coming from his cell. Next, was a question yelled across the room, intended for Elrod. "When am I gettin' the hell out of here?"

Elrod ignored him until the question was repeated, this time louder. "When the fuck am I..."

Elrod rushed toward Hinson's cage, stopping short, apparently to get control of his temper. "You'll get out when the judge says you can. Now, shut the hell up."

Hinson grumbled for a few moments, cursing just enough for me to hear but out of earshot of Elrod, who had returned to his desk.

"Hey, Cantrell, when you gettin' out?" Hinson chuckled at his own cleverness. "May be a long time from what I hear."

"You leave me out of your bullshit, Hinson. I've got nothing to say to you."

"That right? Well, maybe I got somethin' to say to you."

I turned onto my side and raised up on my elbow. "You're fucking with the wrong man, Hinson. My advice to you is that you shut the fuck up now."

"What if I tell you I might know a few things about your pretty little wife? Or is it former wife now?"

I called Elrod. "Get this bastard out of here before he says something I can't let go."

Elrod came to our cages. "Boys, I can't have this bickerin', so the next one that runs his mouth is goin' to the detention center." I realized his threat was not meant for me.

Hinson continued. "I just want this big shot to know that I fucked his wife, and I know a dozen more who done the same."

I held my tongue because I knew Elrod was a man of his word and that Hinson had just bought a one way ticket to the detention center.

Elrod picked up the phone and dialed, but Hinson kept running his mouth. "I spent a month out at your ranch and almost every night in the sack with your old lady."

I listened, wishing I could get my hands around his throat, but determined to let Hinson dig his own grave. I vowed that if I ever ran across the son of a bitch again, I would cripple him for life.

"I wished I was the only one, but she was too much woman for one man. But hell, you already knew that." Hinson rambled on with me taking in every word, adding one more reason each time he spoke for me to break his fucking neck when I got the chance. And I knew I would.

"If you made it worth my while, I might give you some names."

Elrod spoke up. "Hinson, that's all. We've heard enough."

"I just want to give Cantrell one name. You might know him, too, Mr. Deputy. Ever hear the name, Logan Vice? He spent a little time at the Oakwood Ranch, and he don't even have no horse." He laughed.

He sat down on his cot and muttered to himself. I was sure he was relishing the idea that he had gotten in my head and under my skin. But I didn't let on. Fifteen minutes later, two deputies arrived from the detention center and led him toward the door. He looked back in my direction and raised his voice loud enough for me to hear. "Logan Vice ain't even got no horse. I hear tell he is hung like a mule, but he ain't got no horse."

As the doors closed behind him, I made Hinson a silent promise. *You'll get yours, you son of a bitch. I'll personally see that you do.* I had a few other unpleasant thoughts, but they were mostly about Carmen and the company she too often kept. I spent the remainder of Sunday—until I finally fell asleep—remembering how things began between Carmen and me and trying to forget how they ended.

It was 10 a.m. Monday morning when Saperstein arrived at the courthouse. From my cell, I could hear the clamor of television and newspaper reporters who crawled around the entrance to the basement like house lizards. They hurled questions at Saperstein as he stood in the doorway, briefcase at his feet. He was an old hand at fending off innocuous, inane, and redundant questions, and the reporters might as well have been shouting questions at Mount Rushmore. It was plain to see Saperstein was in charge. He raised his hands, quieting the gaggle. "Ladies and gentlemen, after I meet with my client, I may be ready to make a statement. Until then, I will definitely have nothing to say."

I could see Sydney as he made his way to the front desk, where he stopped to sign the visitor's log. He had a malicious grin on his face as he approached my cage, accompanied by the daytime guard. "I'll be damned if it isn't Al Capone!"

"You son of a bitch, Saperstein, where have you been? I'm ready to get the hell out of this place."

The guard opened the cell door and allowed Saperstein to enter. He sat down on the cot. I stood, looking down at the bald spot on the top of his head as he opened his briefcase.

"When am I getting out of here?"

"Today, Delbert, but I have a couple of things to take care of first. You're not charged with speeding, you know."

"Where in the hell you been all morning?"

"Working on things. You've already racked up a fifteen hundred-dollar accounts payable this morning."

"What the hell for? You just got here."

"Been going places and seeing people since seven this morning." He shuffled through his files, came up with a couple of pages and handed them to me. "I have several things in the works. For one, we have a preliminary hearing before Judge James Mansfield at 1 p.m. I've bypassed the magistrate and the bond hearing."

"Why no bond? I need to get out of here."

"You will, but you won't need a bond. The yahoos that arrested you don't have a damn thing to hold you for. So, I'm going to get the charges dropped for now."

"What makes you so sure?"

Well, for one, Judge Mansfield is fair, and second, he thinks the sheriff is a damned buffoon, to say nothing of his understudy, Harlan Haynes."

He got up to leave.

"You leaving me here? "

"Yes. I don't want you in the courtroom running off at the mouth. There is not going to be an arraignment, so you won't have to appear before the judge."

"When do you think I'll be out of here?"

"By four o'clock. I'll be back by then with the judge's order to release you."

"What about an autopsy? I want someone besides that idiot coroner of ours examining Carmen."

"I took care of that and called the medical examiner in Hattiesburg first thing this morning. He'll do a forensic examination tomorrow to determine whether a full-blown autopsy is indicated."

"You charging me for all those calls?"

"You bet your ass," he said. Then Sydney called for the guard to let him out of my cage. The malicious grin returned to his face. "I really hate to leave. These are such fine accommodations."

I decided that at five hundred dollars an hour Sydney was having way too much fun at my expense, so I thought I might give back as good as I was getting. "Hey, Sid, you ever read *A Tale of Two Cities*?"

He looked back at me through the bars. "A long time ago. Why?"

"Well, you may recall a character by the name of Sydney Carton. Ring a bell?"

"Can't say it does."

"Well, he took the place of a condemned man on a cart headed for the guillotine."

"Yeah. What does that have to do with us?"

"You know, you standing in for me in front of the judge and all."

"And what happened to Carton?"

"He got his damned head chopped off. Just hope it doesn't happen to you."

"Pretty good, Delbert. For a desperate man, you still have a sense of humor."

"It's all a front, Counselor, all a front, whistling past the graveyard."

"Keep whistling, Delbert. By the way, tomorrow I'm filing a false arrest suit against the sheriff and his deputy. You don't mind if I spend a few thousand dollars more, do you?"

He walked away still grinning, with me knowing everything he did that day would go on his expense account. I lay back on my cot, waiting for four o'clock, musing about the man who was in the process of saving my ass. *Damn him. He doesn't give two shits about how he spends my money, but that genius is worth every dollar.*

7

WE NEED A PETE PITCHFORK

News reporters from Mobile, Pascagoula, New Orleans, and Hattiesburg lay in wait as Sydney and I exited the courthouse and headed across the driveway to the parking lot. Half a dozen mikes were thrust in my face along with a dozen questions hurled at me from all directions, voices drowning voices. Sydney stopped, holding up his hands to quiet the din.

"Ladies, gentlemen, my client has no statement to make. However, I will attempt to clarify the situation as it now exists. Mr. Cantrell was arrested for something he did not do and for which there is absolutely no evidence. In fact, all charges have been dropped, and I plan to file suit tomorrow on Mr. Cantrell's behalf for false arrest by Sheriff Loudermilk and Deputy Haynes. Just to set the record straight, although Mr. and Mrs. Cantrell were in the process of divorcing, their relationship was entirely amicable. We trust that the authorities will utilize every asset at their disposal to quickly solve the murder of Carmen Cantrell. In that regard, Mr. Cantrell will cooperate fully with authorities to help bring his wife's killer or killers to justice. We will have no other comments or statements until such time as this case is resolved."

A rumble of disappointment from the disgruntled, self-appointed defenders of truth and justice spread from the courthouse doorway to the far reaches of the parking lot. *Can you believe that? The son of a bitch is going to get away with it. Everybody knows he did it.*

Sydney took hold of my arm and ushered me through the throng. Near my truck, he stopped and looked up at me. "Damn, Delbert, go home and get a bath. You smell like hell."

"Well, Counselor, you try wearing the same underwear for three days without a bath and see how sweet your ass smells."

"Seriously, go home, get cleaned up, and get a good night's sleep. We have a lot of work to do. I have some appointments first thing tomorrow but will have everything ready to file your suit before noon in Mansfield's court. We should have the medical examiner's preliminary report by Wednesday. Then, we have to start thinking about finding a murderer. You know suspicion will never go away if we don't."

That realization took the starch out of me for a moment, then I thought about the novel I had just finished reading. "You know what we need, Sid?"

"What?"

"We need a Pete Pitchfork."

He appeared exasperated. "A what? You had better take this seriously. You know you're not out of the woods yet."

"No, no. I mean it. A Pete Pitchfork—a private eye. Those dickheads in the sheriff's department couldn't find their own damn shadow."

"You may be right, Delbert. And I know just the man."

"Who's that?

"Isadore Holt, Holt Security."

"The Black guy who advertises on TV? Calls himself Colonel Holt?"

"Yes, he's done some work for me before."

"He provides security services. What does he know about investigating a murder?"

"Investigating a murder is no different than investigating anything else. Besides, the guy is a lot like you."

"How so?"

"He's got brass balls, Delbert. You two will get along just fine."

IT WAS GOOD TO GET HOME TO A HOT BATH AND CLEAN set of clothes. After a steak dinner prepared by my housekeeper, Josie, I settled back into my recliner and turned the TV on to the evening news, eager to see how the local reporters played up the latest events surrounding Carmen's murder. The station, WBLX Biloxi, began the report by showing a clip of Sydney Saperstein's statement in the courthouse parking lot. The report continued with Sheriff Loudermilk reading a prepared statement asserting that I probably killed Carmen. "Although Delbert Cantrell has been released from custody and charges were temporarily dropped, he remains the number one suspect in the murder of his estranged wife. Our investigation will continue."

The clip also showed the sheriff responding to a number of questions from newspaper and TV reporters. One brave soul broached a question regarding Sydney Saperstein's statement that we intend to sue the sheriff and his deputy for false arrest. He clarified the situation with typical enlightenment. "I ain't never arrested nobody that said he was guilty, but I been in this business long enough to know where there's smoke there's fire."

I scratched my head, wondering what the hell that meant. The fact that Carmen and I were in the process of divorcing apparently was reason enough in his mind to charge me with murder. But I was certain I would not be the only person in Cumbersome County puzzled by the sheriff's comments. If Sid was watching, he would have to be delighted. Josie cleaned the kitchen, then came into my den to let me know she was leaving. She and her husband, Luis, lived in an apartment over the garage behind my house. They were like family to me, especially since Carmen and I separated. "Mr. Delbert, I'm leaving now unless you need something else."

"No, Josie, but tell Luis I'd like to see him first thing tomorrow morning."

I was a little puzzled that she never mentioned Carmen or my three-day stint in the county pokey. Maybe she was concerned about upsetting me, or perhaps Josie had her own suspicions as would many other *friends* of mine. But with Loudermilk and his gang hankering for my scalp, I couldn't worry about what others might suspect.

Sleep came easy and early that night, and I awoke when

the first shreds of daylight found their way into my bedroom. I am by nature, an early riser, ready to eagerly take on each day. This Tuesday morning, I was particularly hyped, the thoughts of Sheriff Loudermilk and Deputy Haynes eating at my gut even before I wiped sleep from my eyes. There was nothing more I wanted than to find some way to hang their asses.

I was going out the back door when I saw Luis coming across the yard. "You want to see me, Boss?"

"Yeah." I kept walking around the side of the house to the front yard, and Luis followed. "I have a busy day ahead and want you to take care of a couple of things. I guess you've seen the front yard where Deputy Haynes dug up the lawn—see if you can repair that. And, when you get a chance this morning, call the Southern Fence Company. I want a steel fence all around the front of the house. Get me some plans and prices by the end of the week."

"How about the backyard fence? You want anything done with it?"

"No, it's fine. That wood fence will last another twenty years. By the way, I want an electric gate in the steel fence, with remotes for the house and vehicles."

"Anything else?"

"Yeah, come to think of it. Check out the sprinkler system and pick up about fifteen bags of fertilizer with weed control. It's that time again."

"I think I used eighteen bags last fall." Luis was a stickler for details.

Not me, I considered myself a big picture guy. "Ok, eighteen, whatever the hell it takes. Just get it done."

"And Boss, I want you to know. I don't blame you if you did it."

"Did what, Luis?"

"You know—kill Miss Carmen. You didn't, did you?" He looked away, his dark eyes avoiding mine.

"No, did you kill her?"

His mouth fell open. "Why would I kill her, Boss?"

"Why would I kill her, Luis?"

"She makes trouble and costs you money."

"Luis, you cost me money, and you make trouble, but I haven't killed you yet."

A broad smile lit up his brown face.

He took off his hat and slapped it against the side of his leg before returning it to his head, a habit I had noted when Luis was fishing for something to say. But so was I. The realization struck me that if Luis and Josie had doubts about my innocence, others would be more certain of my guilt. I hoped my annoyance didn't show, but it probably did. "Get your ass to work, Luis."

"Sure, Boss. I'll take care of everything."

When I drove down the driveway, I saw him in the rearview mirror. He was heading for the storage shed. I knew all traces of Harlan Haynes would be gone from my front yard when I returned that evening. If only Carmen's murder could be as easily resolved.

At half past seven, I pulled my truck into the circle at the ranch. Two flags on poles ruffled above my head, one an American flag, the other the Oakwood Ranch flag—a white background with two quarter horses standing under a cluster of live oak trees. There was little activity, a couple of the horse boarders busy at one of the barns, going back and forth between the watering trough and the stables. A cowgirl I knew as Vicky headed in my direction as soon as I stepped from my truck. Still coming toward me, she pointed at the main barn, which had bright yellow crime scene tape around the entrance.

"Can you do something about that?"

"About what?"

"That tape."

"I just got here. I don't know what's going on." My mind was searching for her last name. Then I remembered Dr. Adams, her ex-husband. She probably kept his name after their divorce.

"Mr. Cantrell, you don't remember me, do you?"

"Yeah, sure I do. You're Vicky Adams."

"You're half right. Vicky Metzger, no longer married to Rod Adams." As an apparent afterthought, she added, "No longer married." She smiled and held out her hand. "I've seen you several times, but we've never been introduced."

The few times I visited the ranch, she was usually tending her horses, two of which were boarded there. I knew very little about her except that she was married to a wealthy chiropractor and owned the best quality quarter horses at Oakwood Ranch. I usually called her *Miss Western Pleasure,* a play on one of the judged events I had watched a few times at the local horse show. It seemed to me there was something about women and horses. The two were a potent sexual combination. I don't believe the cowboys gave two shits about riding horses, but they wanted to be there when the women got out of the saddle.

"Good to finally meet you, Vicky."

"When are we going to be able to get into the tack room? All our saddles and riding gear are in there."

Her question surprised me. I had expected her to tell me how sorry she was to learn of Carmen's death. But if that was on her mind, she was slow to express it.

"I don't know, but I will have my attorney check with the sheriff's department. Have they been here the past couple of days?"

"The sheriff's young son, Josh, comes out every day to feed his dad's horses. He has two that Carmen sold him a couple of months ago."

"No one else?"

"Oh yes, just one officer, but not for long. He was here for a few minutes yesterday."

"Who was that:"

"I don't know his name—a tall guy, young, handsome, looks like he just got out of a tanning booth. I've seen him around here before."

"Probably Logan Vice. Did he hit on you?"

"No." she said. "He's not my type. Too pretty for me."

I strode toward the main barn with her at my heel. Auchtung, Carmen's German shepherd, came rushing from the barn and greeted me with a lick on the hand. "Is he being fed?"

"Yes, I check his feeder every day. He's still good for a couple of days."

When we reached the crime scene tape, we both stopped. She touched my arm. "I'm sorry about Carmen. She was a nice gal—loved these horses. I've been feeding *Skippa My Lu* and *Gold N Silver* for the past three days. I didn't know what else to do since no one was here to take care of them. Her other horses have been left out to graze since Friday. They should be brought in for feeding too."

"I really appreciate you looking after her horses. It would mean a lot to Carmen to know how considerate you are."

She reached up and touched the side of my face. "It was no problem. I know you've been through a lot lately." After a moment, she dropped her arm to her side and shifted her eyes away from mine. I took her actions as kindness without any intention of being flirtatious. But you never know about pampered women used to getting their way. They leave you guessing whether they are truly compassionate or appropriately superficial.

"I'm meeting my attorney first thing this afternoon and will get the main barn open up to boarders, hopefully by feeding time tomorrow morning."

"Good."

"I'll be here this evening. See you then, I guess. Oh yes, before I go, do you know anything about a fight here at the ranch? Police were called?"

"A few months ago, I believe, Gerald Hinson. You know him?"

"I just had the pleasure of spending two nights in lockup with him. He's a jewel."

"Well, Gerald and someone else—I didn't see it, but talk was all over the place, a real knock-down-drag-out I heard."

"You know what the fight was about?"

She hesitated for a moment, apparently picking her words carefully. "I would only be guessing."

"And, Vicky, I bet I can guess better than you."

She appeared uncomfortable, and I apologized for involving her in my affairs.

"Excuse me. I have to let the horses out to pasture." She turned and walked briskly toward the other barn. That was when I noticed how good she looked in her bootcut jeans.

I realized she knew one hell of a lot about the comings and goings at Oakwood Ranch, much more than she was telling me. I called after her. "I will need to talk with you again soon."

She didn't look back.

It occurred to me that I might have misjudged her. *I don't think she warms up a hell of a lot in the saddle.*

8

RIGHT MAN FOR THE JOB

Isadore Holt was not a tall man, Black and burly with a contagious smile. The tan and brown uniform with Eagles on the tips of his collar told me he knew how to play the role of a bird colonel even if he had promoted himself to the position. His eyes didn't just look at me; they pierced holes through the ether between the two of us. His hand grasped mine in an unmistakable assurance: you're dealing with a confident man.

"Isadore Holt. I'm glad to meet you, Mr. Cantrell."

"Likewise."

"Your attorney says you need some help. What can I do?"

"Mr. Saperstein thinks you're the man to help find my wife's killer. I'm sure he brought you up to date on the mess."

"Yeah. Well, as you know I've done some work for him, but I deal mostly with my own folks. Done a couple of murder investigations, but I don't know how I might do sniffing 'round you white folks, 'specially those redneck cowboys."

"Sydney says you've got brass balls. That's good enough for me."

"I hope you understand that by putting me in the middle of this you may be creating problems for both of us. It may get one of us killed."

"That's a chance I have to take. You have a choice. I don't."

"I'm willing, Mr. Cantrell, but I'll tell you what...." He stopped mid-sentence. "You don't mind if I call you Delbert, do you?"

"No problem." I smiled at the thought of a private investigator named *Isadore*, and I wondered what Pete Pitchfork might think. "Do you mind if I call you Isadore?"

"My friends call me *Izzy*, but I prefer Colonel, Colonel Holt. Now, like I was saying, I'll tell you what. You need to see for yourself what we'll be up against. Do you know I'm running for state senator as a Republican? Don't stand a chance in hell of winning, but I'm running anyway."

"Yeah, now it rings a bell. I have seen one or two of your ads. I didn't pay much attention."

"'Cause ain't no way this here nigger goin' get hisself elected." He laughed and shook his head as if he knew exactly what I was thinking.

"I didn't say that."

"No, my man, you probably didn't, but a lot of others did."

"If I felt that way, I wouldn't be here, Colonel. But I would like to know why you're running if you don't believe you can win."

"I'm running because I can. That's an accomplishment in itself."

That was enough to convince me I wanted this man on my team, but he seemed reluctant to commit.

"I'm willing to work with you, but you need to understand the pitfalls before you hire me."

"What pitfalls?"

"Why don't you campaign with me this morning? You'll get an idea what we're up against."

I checked my watch: 9:35. "I got a couple of hours before I meet with Saperstein."

On the drive, I thought of what Isadore Holt might be attempting to do. Sure, he wanted to demonstrate how he would be received by the people who might provide information about Carmen. But he also was testing me. If he was to succeed, he would need my full support. If he was to have my back, I must also have his. If he doubted me, there was no way he would agree to help solve Carmen's murder.

We got into a Holt company vehicle with a large orange star encircled by *Holt Security Company* painted on each front door. Near the farmer's co-op, we stopped, parked the car, and began walking the most prominent neighborhood in the county.

The lady who answered the door of the first house on the block courteously accepted Isadore's pamphlet but did not shake his hand when he offered it to her. Running through my mind was the thought that Colonel Holt would not find much support in that neighborhood. As we continued our canvassing, I began to understand what he encountered his entire life. My thoughts, I am sure, were showing on my face.

He checked his watch. "Cheer up, Delbert. It's only half past ten. We've got a whole half hour to hit pay dirt."

"Damn, Colonel, aren't you tired of having doors shut in your face?"

"Hell, yes, my man, but I'm used to that. It hasn't stopped me yet. Come on, we got people to meet." He took hold of my arm. "I'll find a supporter on this street yet."

At the next house, I stood by the steps while Isadore rang the bell. A bearded fifty-year-old man answered the door. "Can I help you?" The irritation I heard in his voice caused me to step closer in case Isadore needed help.

The colonel didn't flinch. He thrust out his hand. "Are you a Republican?"

"No, if it's any of your business."

Extending a pamphlet in the man's direction, Isadore continued. "I'm Isadore Holt, and I'm running for state senator on the Republican ticket. I'd appreciate your vote."

The man ignored the hand reaching out to him. "I ain't votin' for a nigger."

Isadore's expression didn't change. "My man, I don't blame you. I wouldn't vote for a nigger either. But, you see, I'm not a nigger."

"What do you mean? You're as black as the ace of spades."

"And proud of it—I am a Black man, but I am not a nigger."

The two men stood looking into each other's eyes while I wondered what in the hell might come next. But to my surprise, he extended his hand to Isadore. "I like you, man. You're the kind of sons a bitch we need in Jackson. I'm sure goin' to vote for you."

I sat on the top step, relishing what I had just witnessed, while Isadore patiently explained why he was running for the senate and what he hoped to accomplish if he was elected to the part time job. It made me proud to be with him. Of course, he knew he couldn't win the election, but he had won the moment.

On our way back to the car, I told him how much I admired his perseverance and courage. My earlier life was not easy, but I never faced adversities approaching those of Isadore Holt.

When we got to the car, he opened the trunk and took out a wood stake and hammer.

"What you going to do with that?"

"We'll finish here in a few minutes, but first I have to put one of my signs on the man's front lawn."

"Damn, Colonel, just like Sydney said. You are the right man for the job."

AFTER ISADORE AND I ATE LUNCH AT A SPRAWLING LOG restaurant called Catfish Cabin, he headed back to his office, and I stopped at the ranch to check on things. That's when the enormity of the task that lay in store struck home. Seeing Carmen's dual-wheel Dodge and yellow Jaguar under the carport made me realize how little attention we often pay to things that are right before our eyes. The insignificant becomes important. I wondered if the sheriff or his deputies had examined the automobiles or ranch house for evidence.

Both vehicles were locked. On the front seat of the Jaguar were Carmen's oversized sunglasses. I had the macabre thought that she wouldn't be caught dead without them. If the sunglasses were not on her face, they would be pushed back into her hair. Seeing her sunglasses gave me an eerie sense they had a connection to her last moments alive.

I checked the front and back doors to the house. Both were locked. Looking through a glass panel, I could see through the kitchen into a den area. Nothing appeared to have been disturbed. But Isadore and I needed to get inside for a thorough inspection.

I looked at my watch. It was nearing 1 p.m. After a quick walk around the barns, I drove to my attorney's office.

Sydney Saperstein was busy with another client when I arrived. I took a seat in the lobby and waited. His secretary, Carolyn, a dark-haired southern beauty, brought me a cup of black coffee. "Mr. Saperstein will only be a few minutes. He's going over a will with a client. He has reserved the afternoon for you and wanted to squeeze in the will before you got here."

"How about the lawsuit against Loudermilk? That filed yet?"

"This morning, and the constable has copies for serving on the sheriff and Deputy Haynes. My guess is the subpoenas will be in their hands by late this afternoon."

"Damn, girl, you're good. You know you're going to cost me a dinner one of these evenings."

"Maybe you owe Sydney a dinner. I only do what he tells me."

"Bring him too. I already pay for a lot of his dinners, so it won't matter."

"I know you're not complaining, Mr. Cantrell."

"No, that's for sure. Sid is the best lawyer in this part of the country, but don't tell him I said that."

"God, he doesn't need to be told. He already knows it."

Moments later, Sydney's door opened, and he escorted his client out. He motioned for me to follow him into his office. "Guess Carolyn brought you up to date on the wrongful arrest suit."

"Yes, she's got everything under control, doesn't she?"

"Don't know what I would do without her, By the way, I got a call from Colonel Holt right after lunch. He says you two hit it off. I've asked him to join us this afternoon. He should be here shortly."

"I really liked the man. Think he'll work out fine."

"And the medical examiner called, giving me a heads-up on what he found. The report will go out to the sheriff's department today sometime."

"And?"

"Looks as if this thing is going to get complicated. Your wife..."

"My estranged wife."

"Your wife, it seems, died of asphyxiation, but she was also shot."

I closed my eyes, trying to picture Carmen's last minutes alive. I wondered if she realized she was going to die. If so, she would have accepted it with tranquility. She always seemed to feel safe in the eye of the storm, and whatever came her way, she believed was meant to be.

"She was choked by someone—crushed her larynx. But the examiner found a small caliber gunshot wound in the back of her head. Whoever choked her also shot her for good measure. She was already dead. That's why there was little or no blood evidence. The slug has been sent to a lab in Jackson for analysis."

"That doesn't make sense, Sid. Why didn't the sheriff or coroner find the bullet wound?"

Sid slowly shook his head, disdain for Sheriff Loudermilk evident on his face. He held up his hand. "Who knows?"

If there was one thing I had learned about Sydney Saperstein, it was that he did not suffer fools gracefully. He sat for a moment, apparently gathering his thoughts. "You know something, Delbert, there are a lot of good men and women in this county who could do a fine job as sheriff, but we keep electing idiots. And what choice do we have this time, except two idiots, Loudermilk and Haynes, running for sheriff. Too bad we can't come up with a better candidate."

"Too late for anyone else to file, isn't it?"

"Not too late for a good write-in candidate."

"Anyone you have in mind, Sid?"

"Yes, Colonel Holt, but, hell, he could never get elected in this county."

"I might know someone who could."

"Your friend Elrod Jones?"

"No, Elrod would never do it, but Marge Wilson might. She'd make a great sheriff."

"I don't know Marge Wilson, except that she's a deputy."

"I know her." I gave Sid a shit-eating grin. "We spent Saturday night together."

"Yes, I know all about your sexual exploits over the weekend."

"Kidding aside, Sid, she'd be a tough candidate."

"Take a lot of money, Delbert."

"I've got it."

"You ready to spend a couple hundred thousand?"

"More if I have to. There's nothing I'd like better than to beat the hell out of the sheriff—and that nitwit deputy of his."

He was quiet for a few seconds. "Let's do it, Delbert. I've got a few bucks to kick in."

I reached my hand across his desk, and we shook on it.

A smile crossed his normally implacable face. "Ok, now back to the examiner's report." His smile faded.

"Sid, I still have the question. Why didn't the sheriff see that she had a bullet wound?"

"It would be my guess that he didn't want to see it."

"How about blood? He must have seen that."

"That's the odd part, Delbert. There was no blood. As I said, she probably was already dead when she was shot. The report will clarify that. I'll bet my ass the coroner found that bullet wound but kept it quiet. That worm is in bed with the sheriff."

"Who discovered her body?"

That's still up in the air, but it seems a furrier found her."

"That would be Jason McElroy. He's the one who shoes all the horses at the ranch, fifty-five dollars a shot."

Carolyn called on the intercom. "Colonel Holt is here."

"Show him in."

The door opened. The colonel took a seat next to me. Sydney leaned forward in his chair. "Gents, we have one hell of a task on our hands trying to find the truth about Carmen Cantrell's murder. It won't be easy. I can almost assure you Sheriff Loudermilk will do everything he can to keep you from learning the facts."

Vicky Metzger and her tight-fitting jeans came to mind. "Which reminds me, Sid, the barn is still roped off, and the boarders need access to their tack and saddles. You think you can get the sheriff to complete whatever is left of his investigation so we can get back into the tack room."

"Maybe the son of a bitch will be halfway reasonable, but that's a long shot. On the other hand, it may be good that no one has been allowed to get in there and contaminate the site more than Loudermilk and his deputies already have."

The colonel spoke. "I need to investigate the barn as soon as I can."

"Loudermilk isn't going to like that idea, but I will check with him and let you know." Sydney scribbled on a notepad as he talked. "Too bad you can't do it before the crime scene tape is removed."

I gave Colonel Holt a nod. "We can look around this evening after all the boarders leave."

He smiled. "If the sheriff has no one there, we might get away with it."

Sydney cautioned. "I don't want you to do anything unlawful. But if you intend to, don't ask my legal advice. I will have to caution you against it."

I stood. "Well, Sid, if you're through giving legal advice, there's no use of us sitting here running up my bill with you."

9

COLLECTING EVIDENCE

I went home around five o'clock and called Colonel Holt and confirmed our meeting at the ranch at 7:30. I sat down to watch the evening news but fell asleep and snoozed before the television for almost an hour. When I woke up, Josie had dinner on the table. I invited her and Luis to join me to catch up on the progress Luis had made with Southern Fence Company and to get a feel for anything they might be hearing from their friends. You never know what half-truth you can learn from gossip and rumors, but nothing was said that touched on Carmen's murder or my alleged complicity.

After dinner, I found my spare keys to the ranch house, barns, and outbuildings. My intention was to get into the house where I thought a set of keys for the truck and Jaguar would be. I couldn't stop thinking about Carmen's sunglasses on the front seat of her car. That was not something she would have done. So, someone else must have put them there or she left her car in a hurry.

A Holt Security Company car was pulling into the circle when I arrived at the ranch. The place was nearing early darkness except for security lights at the entrances to the barns. We got out of our vehicles and waited to make certain no one else was on the premises. Auchtung rushed from the barn, growling and baring his teeth. He stopped short when I called his name. We listened again for sounds but heard only an occasional nicker and snort from the horse stalls. After a few moments, we made our way to the back porch. Isadore handed me a pair of plastic gloves. "Put these on. We don't want to contaminate anything."

We entered the house through the kitchen door, turned on the lights, and went from room to room, looking for obvious signs of a struggle. At first blush, everything seemed in place, clean, and orderly. I checked out the kitchen while the colonel went to Carmen's bedroom. I opened the dishwasher. It was empty. Two coffee cups were on the counter with traces of coffee in the bottoms. The Bunn coffeemaker was still turned on. The glass carafe had boiled dry and cracked. It was obvious two people drank coffee that last day of Carmen's life. Coffee was essential to her. She drank it all day long, winter and summer, beginning as soon as she opened her eyes in the morning, until her last cup at bedtime. She must have left the coffeemaker turned on, intending to drink a second cup which she never had the opportunity to do. There was a possibility that the person who shared that last cup of coffee with her was her killer, if not her lover—or maybe both.

I photographed the kitchen counter and the open dishwasher. Under the sink was a box of plastic zip bags. I placed each of the cups and the spoon in separate bags, carefully handling them to preclude contamination. I knew I couldn't risk turning them over to the sheriff, so we would take our evidence to Saperstein and follow his advice. I was certain the medical examiner would have collected DNA material from Carmen's body that could be compared to our evidence. Still, I thought it might be wise to get something from the house that would be certain to contain Carmen's DNA. I went to the laundry room and found a pair of her bikini panties in a hamper. As I slipped them into a separate bag, I couldn't help but think of all the times I had eagerly pulled similar panties down her shapely legs. That thought made me smile at her wickedness. *I hope hers is the only DNA we find on those panties. On second thought, maybe not. The killer's DNA could be on them too.* For the moment, I would keep those thoughts to myself.

"Cantrell, come here." I heard the colonel shout from the master bedroom.

"Look," he said, pointing at the wall behind the wrought iron headboard. "Blood spatter."

I bent down. "Don't see anything."

"Look close, my man." He pointed at a pattern of small red dots on the wall and headboard just above the pillow shams. "Got your camera?"

I pulled out my phone and snapped photographs from several angles, each one showing the colonel's hand pointing out the blood.

"Take a round of shots of the room and the bed." Isadore moved toward the door to keep out of the picture. "That odor tells me there's a lot more blood here." When I finished taking photos, he removed the sham pillows and turned back the comforter. "Whoa," he said, "Look at that, Delbert." He stepped back and pointed to the bloody pillow and sheet. "Get a close-up. It's at least a week old."

My head was spinning. I remembered that the coroner reported Carmen was dead before she was shot, and she bled very little. "Damn, Colonel, guess we're looking at two murders."

"Probably, and if someone was killed in this bed, there is a whole lot more blood someplace." He lifted the corner of the mattress and peered under. "Man, man..." he fell to one knee, crossed himself, then lifted the corner of the mattress again. "Look, Delbert, if you can. It has drained all the way through the mattress."

"I don't think I want to look." I handed my phone to him and held up the corner of the mattress. "You take the pictures."

Isadore tugged at his black tie. "The rotten mother...." That was as close as he ever came to cursing in my presence. "Get another evidence bag, Delbert."

I went to the kitchen and returned with a zip bag.

"Hold up the corner of the mattress again." He took a small penknife from his pocket and cut a blood-stained chunk.

"What do you think happened, Colonel?"

"I think we just stumbled onto another motive for murder. Maybe someone wanted competition out of the way."

"Could be," I said. "Looks like the guy who died here wasn't so lucky in love." As flippant as my words sounded, I was hurting inside. The thought that I was probably standing by the bed in which Carmen made love for the last time affected me in a way I didn't expect. I had believed I was over her for good, but my stone heart was telling me that wasn't so.

Isadore aimed the phone at the small hole he had just carved into the bottom of the mattress. I left the room while he made the bed as if it had never been disturbed.

SPARE KEYS TO THE VEHICLES WERE ON A HOOK BY THE kitchen door. We turned out the lights and closed and locked the door after us.

"Let's get a look inside that Jaguar, Colonel."

As we walked around the house to the front driveway, Auchtung came growling from his sentinel spot inside the barn. I called his name and he came to me, wagging his tail. "You hungry, boy? I'll come to the barn and fill your feeder in a few minutes. Go on now." I pointed toward the barn, and he headed in that direction.

I unlocked the car door with the remote, and Isadore pulled it open, still wearing plastic gloves. "I wonder if they took fingerprints, Delbert."

"Probably not, but what do you expect from that yokel we call a sheriff. You know damn well he doesn't have anyone qualified to do that, and he sure as hell didn't ask for help. He just sent Harlan Haynes to haul me in."

"Delbert, I haven't asked, but you know I have to. You didn't have anything to do with this, did you?"

"Do you think Sydney Saperstein would be putting his neck out if he thought I did?"

"You can't ever tell about attorneys. If the fee is right,

they'll take Charlie Manson for a client. Like I said, I had to ask the question."

"Well, you have my answer. Colonel, if there is any doubt in your mind, I'll not hold a grudge if you leave right now."

He slapped me on the back. "Shine that flashlight around. I can't see much inside the car."

"We might have to wait until morning to get a better look. But see if her .32 is in the door panel. She always kept it there."

"Nothing here."

"Check under the driver's seat."

He bent over and pulled a small handbag from under Carmen's seat and handed it to me. "This look like your wife's?"

A small wallet was inside, containing credit cards and her driver's license. "She wouldn't have left these."

"You know her, Delbert. What do you think happened?"

I knew the colonel was thinking about all the people coming and going at the ranch, but the one thing that made me realize both murders happened after dark was the sunglasses Carmen left in the car. Otherwise, they would have been on her forehead.

"It must have happened in the evening or during the night. Let me try this on you, Colonel. "When she drove up, she must have heard the commotion going on inside the house and ran to see what was happening. Whoever killed the person in her bed caught her by surprise and choked her unconscious."

"You may be right. And after she saw what had

happened, he knew he had to finish her off. But why did she end up in the tack room?"

"I don't have an answer for that unless he intended to hide her body or bury it on the ranch someplace. It may indicate some regret for killing her."

"But what I don't understand is why he would spend time cleaning her up if he was going to dispose of her. And what happened to the body of the bleeder in the bedroom?"

"Your guess is as good as mine, but I don't think he intended to kill her. There was just no way he could let her live. After he choked her, there was no alternative. He probably spent a lot of time, maybe hours, trying to figure out what to do with their bodies. At least he cared enough about Carmen to clean her up. I assume the other corpse was left here in the back of a truck in a bloody mess."

"I think we're on the right track, Delbert. Let's check the tack room and see what we find."

AUCHTUNG GROWLED AGAIN AS WE NEARED THE BARN. When we were under the security light, he went back to his house near the door to the tack room.

We ducked under the yellow tape. I pulled out a ring of keys and opened the tack room door. Ollie, the barn cat, darted across the room in front of us. Colonel Holt jumped back, his hand going to his holster. We both laughed, but only for a few seconds, as the gravity of the moment fell over us.

"You know what just occurred to me, Colonel?"

"What's that?"

"If she was murdered at night, her killer must have been someone who spent a lot of time here at the ranch, someone Auchtung was familiar with. Otherwise, he would have chewed off the damn guy's leg."

"Does he bother the regular boarders?"

"No, in fact, he ignores everyone during the day. But at night, he goes after anything that makes a noise. And if he doesn't know you, he may bite a hole in your throat."

"Thanks," he said. "I'll make sure I don't come out here without you."

A chalk outline on the floor showed where Carmen's body was found. It was behind a dozen or more bales of hay and feed sacks marked with the names of Oakwood boarders. No wonder Vicky and others were bitching. They had not been able to access their riding tack or feed for at least four days. I made a promise to myself to get that restriction lifted the next day.

We looked carefully around the floor of the tack room but found no trace of blood or anything that might indicate she was murdered where her body was found.

"What do you think, Colonel?"

"There is a possibility that she ran from her killer and hid here in the tack room, but I doubt it. I think she was killed in the house and carried out here."

"Try this on for size. The killer might have spent a whole day in the house trying to figure out what to do with the body without being seen by anyone. I think he eventually decided to dispose of her somewhere out on the pasture, maybe in the backwoods. He brought her here, intending to throw her body across one of the horses and carry her out to the watering hole. He heard someone drive up, dumped her here, and hauled ass across the pasture without being seen."

"Sounds reasonable, Delbert. Let's take our evidence to Mr. Saperstein tomorrow. No use telling him we crossed the crime scene tape. He doesn't need to know that."

"There's something else I thought about."

"What?" The Colonel was wide-eyed and listening.

"The killer must not have driven a car to the ranch. Either that or our theories are way off track."

"Why do you say that?"

"If he escaped through the woods, he would have left his car behind, wouldn't he, Colonel?"

"Unless he had help. Maybe he hid and waited for someone to give him a ride."

"You know what, Colonel, I think we're looking for an accomplice too."

I filled Auchtung's automatic feeder. No use worrying about water with all the horse troughs around the barn and in the paddock.

We turned out the lights and locked the door. The clues needed to solve Carmen's murder would not be found in the tack room. But, for certain, someone who knew her and the ranch very well was her killer.

10

ANOTHER TWIST

At home that night, I sent the pictures from my phone to my computer and printed two copies. Afterward, I copied the file to a thumb drive as a permanent record. I marked the photos and evidence bags with a title, location, date, and time.

Colonel Holt and I met the next morning at Saperstein's office. He had only a few minutes to spare before a court appearance. We told him our theories and gave him the samples we had collected.

"When I get back from court, I'll contact Dr. Schmidt at the forensic lab in Jackson. We'll get them started on the DNA as soon as possible. Carolyn can run it up to them tomorrow. It may take two or three weeks before we get it back. I think we can hold off informing the sheriff until then without being accused of withholding evidence. Until we hear from the lab, we won't know if we have real evidence or not. We may just have some soiled panties and dirty dishes in our possession."

"Any reason why I can't have access to the ranch house and vehicles?"

"Good reasons—lots of them, but it's your house, and they are your cars. Legally, you're free to do as you wish for now, Delbert, but you may have blood evidence in the bedroom that needs to be protected. You've already documented the date and time you discovered it, so we'll wait until we have the DNA results before notifying authorities. But I recommend waiting for state investigators to inspect the house and automobiles before you reenter them."

"'We probably need to post a guard out there," Colonel Holt said. "Delbert, if you know someone you can trust, that should be fine. Otherwise, I can station a person there, at least at night."

"Go ahead and post your night guard, but I think I know a good man to look after things. I may offer him a job today."

Saperstein opened his briefcase and inserted files as he spoke. "That sounds like a good idea. Who do you have in mind? Your friend, Elrod Jones?"

"Yes. He needs to get the hell away from Loudermilk."

"Speaking of the sheriff, we'll have to inform him you've taken possession of the ranch, and we want the crime scene released for your boarders. That should cause him apoplexy."

"Can you do that this morning? Maybe apoplexy will kill the son of a bitch by this evening."

That brought a grimace from Sydney and a chuckle from the colonel.

"I'll have Carolyn take care of that."

We walked to the elevator and parking lot together.

"Gents, unless something new arises, I don't think we need to get together tomorrow. Let's schedule a meeting for Friday, say 1 p.m."

"Fine," Isadore and I said almost simultaneously.

"If my schedule changes, I'll give both of you a call."

The two of us stood chatting as Saperstein backed out of his parking space. He lowered the window for one last comment. "I hope you're thinking about funeral plans. I expect the medical examiner to release the body today or tomorrow. I will let you know as soon as I hear." He then pulled away, leaving me to ponder the grim task of arranging Carmen's funeral.

The colonel shook my hand. "You've got a lot to take care of, so let me know if I can help you." He repeated his offer and added, "Anyway at all."

"I have it under control, my friend. You know as well as I that life goes on, and we have to do the best we can with it."

The colonel was still grasping my hand. "I have to get back on the campaign trail for a little while, then start talking to Miss Carmen's friends to see which one of them did her in. How about you?"

"I'm going up to my construction site in Leakesville. If I don't raise hell with my foreman every so often, he tends to slow down. After that, I am going to start my own election campaign."

The colonel must have believed I was joking. "What are you running for, Delbert?"

"Nothing, but I'm willing to spend a wad on the candidate who can kick Loudermilk's ass."

"Anyone special in mind?"

"You would be my first choice, Colonel, but I need

someone who can beat our illustrious sheriff and his nitwit deputy."

"You going to get Elrod Jones to run?"

"No. Marge Wilson if she will do it."

"I've never met her."

"Tough lady."

I could see the disappointment in his face, but I had sized him up as a realist. He must have known he could never win an election for sheriff in Cumbersome County, and I was sure he would agree the election was too crucial to lessen our chances of winning. But just like his run for the state senate, he would have given the campaign for sheriff his best effort. I wished things could have been different, but I am a realist, too.

"Can I count on your support, Colonel?"

"Yes, of course. And Delbert, I'll help her get every Black vote in the county."

"Tell you what, Isadore. I'm going to buy you twenty-five thousand worth of TV ads for your senate campaign."

"Thanks, Delbert, but you will just be wasting your money."

"No, no. Your time is more valuable than my money, and you don't think you're wasting your time even if you lose."

I offered him my hand.

He grasped it and embraced me with tears in his eyes.

THE MEN WERE ON BREAK WHEN I ARRIVED IN Leakesville. My foreman was nowhere in sight. The men scrambled for their tools and equipment as soon as I got out of my company truck. "Where in the hell is Campbell?" I yelled in the direction of several workers scurrying toward the black-and-red backhoe.

When they didn't respond, I put two fingers to my lips and spit out a shrill whistle. Everyone on the site stopped and looked in my direction.

"Where in the hell is Campbell?" I directed my repeated question to a worker we called Dooley. He was the second man in charge and was apparently carrying the load for Cecil Campbell. He walked toward me, not saying anything until he was two feet away.

"Boss man, Cecil ain't been on the job since last Thursday, and I don't know where in the hell he is. I've called his home and cell phone, but can't get an answer."

"Why didn't you call me?"

"At first, I didn't think anything about it. Then, when I couldn't get him on the phone, I thought about callin' you but didn't want to get him in trouble. I told the guys this mornin' if Cecil didn't show up today, I was drivin' down to talk things over with you."

"You guys are supposed to be pouring foundations today, and Cecil's ass is laying out."

"The forms are all ready now, Mr. Cantrell."

"How long you been with me, Dooley?"

"Five years. Why?"

"You've been with me long enough to call me Delbert. Now, tell me where Campbell said he was going when he left work Thursday."

"He didn't say. He left here in the truck a few minutes after you did Thursday afternoon."

"If you hear from him, tell him I said to get his ass down

to my house and explain where in the hell he's been. Now, how about the foundations?"

"The concrete trucks are scheduled to come startin' at one o'clock this afternoon. It will take today and all day tomorrow, but we'll be on time. I need to talk to you about orderin' materials. When can I do that"?"

"Tomorrow. I'll come by to check on the foundations."

I headed to my truck, then stopped and looked back at him. "Thanks, Dooley, for carrying the load. I'll make it up to you."

He held up his hand and walked toward me. "Just a minute, Boss. There are a couple of things I need to tell you."

I waited for him to catch up to me. "Yeah, what is it?"

"About Cecil." He hesitated then continued. "I know you been through hell, but you need to know. I'm sorry I didn't say somethin' before this."

"Yeah?"

"I think Cecil had somethin' goin' with your ex."

I was stunned for a moment, not because Carmen might have been screwing Cecil, but because he would carry on with her behind my back. I always treated the man like a brother, taught him the construction business, and paid him very, very well. Besides, he was married to a beautiful woman and had two kids. "That son of a bitch. Wait 'til I see him again."

I continued walking toward my truck with Dooley a half step behind. "I'm sorry, Mr. Delbert. I really am."

"Hell, I wouldn't be sorry if I were you. You just got yourself a twenty thousand dollar a year raise."

"I appreciate that, but that's not why I told you."

"And that's not why you're getting a raise. You now

have Campbell's job, and when I find his truck, you'll have that too. Now get your ass to work and earn your pay. I'll bring one of the design engineers from Peterson Engineering with me to go over the plans with you tomorrow. Be ready to ask and answer questions. You have to carry the load because, right now, I have too many other irons in the fire. And if Campbell shows up, tell him he's fired."

"I got it, Boss. You can count on it." He turned and ran toward the workers.

I knew he was one happy man. Too bad so many others weren't, including me.

ON MY WAY BACK HOME, I CALLED ELROD JONES ON HIS cell phone. He was working the day shift patrolling the eastern half of the county. "Yeah," he said." I'll be heading in your direction about four. What do you want to talk to me about?"

"I want to make you an offer you can't refuse."

"Doin' what?"

"Running Oakwood Ranch."

"What the hell do I know about show horses?"

"You know how to feed them, don't you? And you for damn sure, know how to mend fences and sow winter rye."

"I'll have to think about it, Delbert. I don't make much as a deputy, but I have job security and a pretty good health plan."

"You need to hear my offer. So, stop by and see me on your way home."

"OK, Del should be there close to five, but I doubt that I'm interested."

"We'll see—oh, and Elrod, give Marge Wilson a call. I need to talk with her. I'll be home in another half hour. You have my number there, don't you?"

"Yeah, I got it in my cell. You going to offer her a job as a ranch hand, too?"

"No, Elrod. I'm going to get her elected sheriff."

I heard him laughing just as he lost the signal or maybe shut off his phone, probably believing I had lost my mind.

OVER BEER AND NACHOS SUPREME, I PITCHED AN OFFER to Elrod that he couldn't refuse, but he was a hard sale.

"Delbert, in spite of my bitchin', I really like my job. Ain't hard, maybe a little monotonous at times, but I get to interact with a lot of different folks, and I like that."

"And you look damn good in your uniform."

He laughed because he knew I had seen right through him. "Yeah, I guess I like that image. I know my wife does."

"And you like kissing Loudermilk's ass just to keep your job." I wanted to convince him to come on with me before I talked about dislodging John Loudermilk from his perch. If Marge Wilson won, I would no longer have that argument.

"You know me better than that, Delbert. I ain't ever kissed nobody's ass—kicked a few, but kissed? No."

"Don't get your ass in the air, Elrod, I was just making a point. John Loudermilk is an asshole. They couldn't pay me enough to work for him."

A typical Elrod Jones mischievous smile crossed his face.

"I thought you were goin' to get Marge Wilson elected. If you did, I wouldn't have to put up with John."

It was time to get down to the nut cutting. "How much do you make a year?"

"Twenty-seven, plus benefits."

"I'll pay you twice that."

Elrod's eyes widened. "I ain't worth that much."

"The problem is you don't know what you're worth."

"Delbert, I appreciate your offer, but I have to think about it. Give me a couple of days."

"No, Elrod, I'm running out of time. You say you're not worth fifty thousand, but you don't realize how much being able to trust someone is really worth. And right now, I need to surround myself with people I can trust."

"All right," he said. "Tell me what I'll be doin'."

"You'll be running the ranch, dealing with boarders, making sure horses get fed, groomed, and exercised."

"I don't know anything about that."

"You'll learn."

We shook hands.

"Oh yes, Elrod, you'll be living in the ranch house as soon as Carmen's investigation is closed."

"How big is that house? I've never been inside."

"Four bedrooms, three baths, plenty of room for your three kids."

Smiling broadly, he shook my hand again. "Can't wait to tell Louise."

I walked with him to the door. "Think you can start in a week?"

"I'll start right now working on my off time. But I have to

give two weeks' notice to the sheriff. It ought to frost his ass when he learns I'm goin' to work for you."

"Sounds good, Elrod. I'll get Saperstein to draw up a contract."

As I closed the door behind Elrod, my cell phone rang. It was Marge Wilson.

11

HOLD THE PRESSES

The phone rang. "Cantrell Construction."

"Delbert?"

"Yeah, Marge. I've been expecting your call."

"How can I help you?"

"The first thing I want to do is thank you for the meatloaf. It sure as hell beat stale bologna sandwiches."

"You know you were welcome, but is that really why you wanted me to call?"

"No, ma'am. Fact is, I want to make you an offer you can't refuse."

"Try me, Delbert. I've had a lot of those in my day, and thankfully, I've refused most of them." She laughed. "My husband is happy about that too."

"Seriously, Marge, I have a very important proposal."

"Let's hear it, Delbert. The least I can do is listen."

"How would you like to run for sheriff?"

There was total silence on the line, not even a crackle

from the phone for several seconds before she spoke again. "Are you drinking, Delbert?"

"As a matter of fact, I am. I'm on my second beer but still have all my faculties."

"You are joking though, right?"

"No, Marge, listen. I am willing to spend whatever it takes to mount a campaign. I know we can do it. I already have a corner on every Black vote in the county. All we need is 30 percent of the whites."

"Sounds like too big a risk. What if I lose? I need this job."

"You won't lose, Marge. We'll run ads every hour on all three local TV channels and every fifteen minutes on a half dozen radio stations, and half-page ads in the papers every day for the next six weeks."

"That'll cost a fortune, Delbert."

"Maybe a quarter million, but I don't give a damn as long as we beat Loudermilk and Haynes.

"It's too late for me to get on the ballot."

"I know, but we'll have the biggest write-in campaign this county has ever seen."

"You really think we can do it?"

"You bet your ass, Marge."

"You know I can't do anything like that without talking it over with Ralph."

"I'll bet he won't stand in your way."

"Delbert, if Ralph agrees, you've got yourself a candidate."

"Give me a call after you've talked with him. If he says it's OK with him, we'll call for a news conference tomorrow. Let me know tonight so I can call the news outlets as soon as possible. Those lizards will think I've got an announcement to make about Carmen's murder. They won't miss a chance to hear a confession from me right there on the courthouse steps. You and Ralph be there, and we'll spring the announcement of your candidacy on them."

"You know, if I do this, I'll get every shit detail the sheriff can dream up."

"Don't worry, Marge. If it all goes to hell, I'll give you a job."

"I'm in, Delbert. I just don't know about Ralph. He isn't much of a risk-taker."

"I'll bet you've been able to get him to see things your way before, and I'm counting on you now. It's about time this county had an honest sheriff."

I have always known that wherever a television crew truck stops, a crowd gathers. So, the first thing I did was to notify the television stations in Biloxi, New Orleans, and Mobile that I was about to make a blockbuster announcement on the courthouse steps. Next I called the local newspaper editors and those in Jackson, Hattiesburg, and New Orleans. We set up our microphones and amplifiers as announced. The three-piece bluegrass band I hired began to play, attracting a crowd. As the reporters assembled at the foot of the steps, curiosity seekers gathered behind them, swelling the numbers to at least fifty people. Marge was on the top stoop next to me, looking serious and lovely in her navy blue pants suit and red blouse. Ralph stood next to her, wearing his Sunday best. At exactly 11 a.m., I approached the mike, ready to launch into a tirade against Sheriff Loudermilk before introducing Marge Wilson as our next sheriff of Cumbersome County.

The sheriff and three deputies approached me from behind the crowd. At the top of the steps, Loudermilk attempted to address the crowd using my main microphone. I signaled to my sound man with a forefinger across my throat. He killed the power to the microphones in the sheriff's speech mid-sentence. Loudermilk turned to me, speaking at the top of his voice, "Mr. Cantrell, this is an unlawful assembly, and I am orderin' you to cease and desist."

"What law am I breaking, Sheriff?"

"I don't know, but you can't assemble on the courthouse steps without a permit."

I supposed there might be an ordinance against a demonstration without a license, but I wasn't demonstrating. I knew damn well that if there was such an ordinance, the sheriff wouldn't have any idea what it was. And I was determined to prove it. "What law prohibits that?"

"I don't know, but I know you can't do it."

"Sheriff, I am not demonstrating. I just intend to make an announcement of interest to many people in this county."

"Mr. Cantrell, I am ordering you to end this unlawful assembly now. If you are not gone in five minutes, we will confiscate your equipment."

I picked up my microphone and called out to my sound man. "Carl, take the amplifiers and mikes across the street to the John Deere parking lot. The owner won't mind. I buy a lot of equipment from him."

Ten minutes later, we were set up, and my company

truck had been driven onto the lot. I helped Marge onto the truck, then Ralph and I climbed aboard. By then, the crowd had increased considerably. I raised the microphone close to my chin and began.

"I have an announcement for the citizens of Cumbersome County, which, I trust, you news folks will deliver in its entirety. I have long suspected that our sheriff's department, headed by John Loudermilk, is corrupt. I am aware that many of our citizens have complained of corruption and infringement on basic rights by the sheriff and many of his deputies.

"Well, now I can tell you, from firsthand experience, those complaints are well founded. Most of you are aware that my estranged wife, Carmen Cantrell, was murdered last week. Sheriff Loudermilk, rather than doing a thorough investigation, chose to send his deputy, Harlan Haynes, to arrest me for a murder I did not commit and for which there was absolutely no evidence to warrant an arrest. In fact, the arrest was so baseless, my attorney filed a motion to dismiss in court, requesting that all charges be dropped. And as many of you know, that motion was granted. I now have a false arrest suit pending against the sheriff and Deputy Haynes."

From the side of my eye, I watched Sheriff Loudermilk and his deputies standing on the courthouse steps. I could imagine he remained there because he wondered what in the hell his deputy, Marge Wilson, was doing alongside me as I blasted the department of which she was a part. I continued.

"I have learned that I cannot depend on our sheriff to solve my wife's murder, so I have begun my own investigation with the help of a professional detective. We are making progress but cannot expect the cooperation of Sheriff Loudermilk in solving the crime of the decade here in our county.

"Because of the corruption, dishonesty, and ineptness of the sheriff's department, I believe it is time to elect a sheriff that will clean up that department and give us the type of police protection we deserve. As you know, we have only one announced candidate opposing John Loudermilk and that is his deputy, Harlan Haynes.

"Now, let me assure you that I think Deputy Haynes is less corrupt than John Loudermilk, but not by much. In many ways, I am sure he is well meaning, but that is not good enough for the citizens of this county. We need someone who has not been influenced by the current sheriff, someone who is honest to the core, someone we can truly depend on to make the sheriff's department one of the best in the state of Mississippi. That person is the lady standing next to me here on the bed of my truck. That lady is Deputy Sheriff Marge Wilson."

I stepped back and beckoned Marge to the microphone. She appeared a little nervous, taking time to grasp the seriousness of the moment. But when she launched into her initial campaign statement, I was confident we were seeing our next sheriff. Looking at the notes in her hand, she began.

"I want everyone to know that this is the very first time I have ever thought of running for sheriff or any other public office. I don't pursue the sheriff's job to satisfy any personal ambition. I am doing it because I have been witness to many of the injustices Mr. Cantrell has just talked about.

"It will be a difficult campaign, causing many personal problems for both me and my husband, Ralph, who has always backed me in every personal endeavor I have taken on. I pursue this now with full confidence that Ralph will be with me all the way through the campaign.

"Now, I want to talk about the election process. I'm sure you know it is too late to get my name on the ballot for the election, which is less than six weeks away. I will depend entirely on write-in ballots. If anyone decides to vote for me, they will need to spell my name correctly. That is Marge Wilson, M-a-r-g-e W-i-l-s-o-n. Voters can also simply write *M. Wilson.*"

I leaned in and whispered to her. "Let them know you will commence your ads tomorrow and will purchase time on the local TV to show people how to fill out the ballot with your name written in."

She turned back to the microphone. "I should also tell you that, during my campaign, I will continue doing my job as a deputy to Sheriff Loudermilk, and I will give him the loyalty he should have as our sheriff, at least until January. By the way, I will soon have a TV spot, showing people how to write my name on the ballot." She was smiling as she stepped back from the mike.

I turned to her husband. "Would you like to say anything, Ralph?"

He leaned into the mike without moving from his position alongside Marge. "Folks, this is a wonderful woman. I know 'cause I been with her for nearly thirty years. And anybody who could put up with me that long would have to be a saint. Marge Wilson will make you folks a great sheriff."

I pulled the mike a few inches closer. "I want to thank everyone for listening to what we had to say. For those of you who came to hear my confession of murder, I'm sorry to disappoint you. But I'm sure you'll agree Marge Wilson's announcement that she is running for sheriff is more important than any false confession could be. The best thing we can do for the people of this county is to elect her our sheriff."

12

THE WEB WIDENS

When I got back home, there were three messages on my answering machine. Dooley and the colonel asked me to return their calls. The message from Sid Saperstein was succinct and direct. "Delbert, for a bright man, you can do some dumb things. Call me."

I knew Saperstein's first question was going to be, "Why in the hell didn't you call me before going down to the courthouse and tweaking John Loudermilk's nose?"

And my answer was going to be, "Because I knew damn well you would advise me against it."

But I dialed him just to make sure I knew him as well as I thought. He answered the phone. "Saperstein here."

I toyed with him. "Where's Carolyn?"

"You dumb son of a bitch."

"What'd I do, Counselor?"

"That's the problem, Delbert. You forget that I am your counselor."

"What'd I do?"

"I just watched some breaking news of an idiot down by the courthouse tugging on Superman's cape. And you know damn well I would have advised you against it."

"Well, first thing, Sid, I wouldn't characterize him as Superman, more like Underdog. Second, I would have done it anyway, even if you had recommended against it."

"Okay, Delbert, but one of these nights, you're going to end up in a dog cage in the basement of the courthouse, and I'm going to leave your ass there for a month before I bail you out."

"I love you too, Sid. But why isn't your secretary answering the phone?"

"Because I don't have a secretary right now. Carolyn's on her way back to the office from Jackson. Remember I told you she was taking your evidence to the crime lab up there. You need her for something?"

"No, Sid, I just thought business might be so bad you had to let her go."

Sid chuckled, muttering something I didn't understand. But I was sure that somewhere in his rant was the Yiddish word for idiot or worse. "No, Delbert, as long as you keep stepping in shit, I can afford Carolyn and four more like her. Keep up the good work, my friend."

I had a feeling that in spite of his obvious irritation, Sid admired me for not having to kiss anyone's ass. While I sensed an advantage, I pressed. "Is that the only reason you called me?"

"Main reason, but I also wanted to let you know Carmen's body will be released tomorrow. I've instructed the examiner to return her to Salvation Funeral Home. You have to decide about arrangements."

"Sid, I have to notify her mother and sister in Little Rock before I do anything. But I intend to have her cremated unless her family objects. And I don't think they will. That relationship was not good."

"You need to hold off on cremation until we have the results back from the crime lab. That's probably three weeks away."

"I guess so. But I hate to leave her body with that goddamn pervert, Palmer Lovett, for three weeks."

"I think those are unfounded rumors. I hear the same thing about all undertakers. You can't believe what you hear."

"I'll take your word for it, Sid, but for an attorney, you're pretty damn naive about some things. Oh, before I forget, are we meeting tomorrow?"

"No, let's do it Monday. I'm tied up tomorrow."

"OK, Colonel Holt and I will see you Monday. Say 1 p.m.?"

"That's fine. I'll call if there's a change. By the way, Delbert, I think you're backing a winner in Marge Wilson."

I CALLED ON THE INTERCOM AND ASKED JOSIE TO WHIP UP something for lunch. I am not normally a breakfast eater, and it was way past lunchtime. "Make me a small salad and—you have any of that vegetable beef soup you made a couple of days ago?"

"Yes," she said, "If Luis didn't sneak into it."

"If he has, he's fired."

I believed she thought I meant it. "Oh no, Mr. Cantrell, I was just kidding. Are you eating in the dining room?"

I guessed she was saving the soup for Luis, so. I enjoyed the moment. *Hell, let him eat cake.* "No, I'll have it in here. I've got some work to do."

While I waited for her to bring lunch to my office, I called Dooley's cell phone.

"Yeah, Dooley, what's going on?"

"We're about through pouring foundations. Got three more truck loads due in the next hour. Are you and the engineer comin' up here this afternoon?"

"Yes, I'm picking him up at 2:30, and we'll be there a little after three. You heard anything from Campbell?"

"No, Boss, I called his wife this mornin' and either she's coverin' for him, or she's got no idea where he is."

"Has she heard from him at all?"

"Accordin' to her, not since last Thursday."

After lunch, I left a message for Isadore, telling him I would call later, then went to the company office to meet with my equipment manager, Eddie Mayfield, to see if Campbell had turned in his truck.

"No, Delbert, and that truck is due for maintenance— 40,000-mile checkup. He runs the shit out of it between oil changes, so I'm not surprised he hasn't brought it in."

"It's more than that, Eddie. The son of a bitch has skipped town with my truck. He hasn't been on the job for a week."

"Hasn't called in?"

"No, and his wife says she doesn't know where he is."

"It don't have anything to do with Miss Carmen's murder, does it?"

Damn, I thought, *the husband is always the last to find out.* "What do you know about that?"

"Nothing, really, just heard rumors. I think Cecil was bragging a little to some of the men."

"Well, if he was bragging, he was a real dumb ass, 'cause that's a pretty good way to get yourself killed. And it just might have happened."

"Damn, Boss, you didn't do anything to him, did you?"

"Eddie, I wouldn't waste my time. Carmen and I were getting a divorce, and I didn't give a damn who she was fucking. But sounds to me like Campbell was in some pretty tight competition for her favors."

"What are you going to do about your truck?"

"I'll need for you to get the registration, VIN, etc. and report the truck misappropriated. We can't claim it was stolen because it was assigned to him. I'll get Elrod Jones to come out and take down all the information. He'll get a BOLO issued."

"Wonder where Cecil is?"

"Dead, I hope."

"You don't mean that do you, Delbert?"

"You bet your ass, Eddie. I don't like it when someone fucks me over. Fucking with Carmen is one thing, but stealing my truck is a whole other bucket of worms."

"I'll remember that, Boss."

"Eddie, I want you to get a truck ready for Dooley. He's taking Campbell's place."

"I don't know what I've got that I can let go of right now."

"Buy him a new one then. A Ford off-road."

"Hell, let me give him mine, and I'll get a new one. Mine only has 55,000 miles on it."

"Ok, you conniving asshole." I slapped him on the back and walked toward my truck.

He followed. "I really appreciate it, Delbert. Where are you headed now?"

"Up to Leakesville to check on the foundations. They're supposed to be finished today."

"You've got a lot of things to take care of right now. Let me know if I can help you at the construction site. I have everything pretty well under control here."

"Thanks, Eddie; it may come to that. I'll let you know. By the way, watch the evening news tonight and grab a newspaper on the way home. Some things are happening that you may be interested in."

Colonel Holt called me back while I was on the way to Leakesville with the engineer. "We still meeting with your attorney tomorrow?"

"No, Colonel, Monday at 1 p.m. Have you assigned anyone to watch the ranch?"

"Yes, he goes on your payroll tonight at 6 p.m. I'm billing him to you at thirty an hour. Any problem with that?"

"It's OK, I guess. You paying him fifteen?"

"I could tell you that, Delbert, and make you feel good,

but truth is, I'm paying him twelve-fifty. I can hire good men for that all day long."

"I'd rather pay fifteen and know I can trust him."

"Well, I got you a good man out there, a preacher."

"Hell, Colonel, they're the worse ones, but he works for you, so I assume he can be trusted."

"You got my word on it."

"That's good for me—you heard anything about Marge Wilson running for sheriff?"

"Not yet. Has she announced?"

"This morning at the courthouse. Our ads start tomorrow on all three TV channels and in the *Crier*. But watch the news this evening. I think you'll like what you see."

"Delbert, I just wanted to bring you up to date on what I've been doing. I ran into Deputy Logan Vice over at the interstate rest area. I stopped to take a leak, and he was parked there with some blonde woman. It was just getting dark, but I could see two people in a white sedan. It looked like they were making out. I thought it was a police officer because he was wearing a uniform cap, but his patrol vehicle was nowhere in sight."

"You probably know, Vice is one piece of shit. Did you speak to him?"

"Yes, he didn't have any choice. Just as I came out of the restroom to get in my car, another officer pulled up in a sheriff's car. Vice and I came face-to-face, three feet apart. He looked startled but spoke to me."

"How'd you know it was Vice?"

"I've seen him around, and of course, he knows my vehicles." He chuckled. "And I'm the only Black colonel in this county, so he sure as heck knows me."

"What do you think he was doing?"

"Well, if you really want my opinion, and to put it bluntly, I would say he was getting his knob polished. Why else would he be parked at the rest stop in some woman's car?"

"What did he say?"

"He was grinning like hell, like he was proud of himself. He just said 'How's it goin', Colonel?' then hopped in the police car with his buddy, and they hauled ass, burning rubber right onto the freeway."

"Some gal's husband is going to take care of his ass one of these days. Anything else on your mind?"

"Yes, as a matter of fact..."

Another call came in on my phone. "Give me a minute, Colonel. I have a call I need to take. Let me call you back."

It was Elrod. "Delbert, I'm just letting you know, they've found a burned-out white Ford truck off Highway 57. Has your markings on it. I'm headin' out there now."

"Where on 57?"

"Not too far from old Highway 63."

"I'm just south of there now, heading for Leakesville. Who's on the scene right now?"

"I don't know. I guess the guy who found the truck."

"A hunter?"

"Don't know that either. And, Delbert, I understand there's a body in the truck, burned too bad to tell if it's a man or woman."

"I've got a good idea it's a man."

"Anyone I know?"

"I don't think you know him. I think it's my foreman, Cecil Campbell. He and his truck are missing."

"Yeah, damn, I know Cecil. I went to school with him. Anyway, I got to go, Delbert. See you out there."

I called Colonel Holt. "I need you on a possible murder scene. Meet me at Highway 57 and old Highway 63 as soon as you can. I'll be parked on 57, going toward State Line."

I called Dooley and told him to put my visit on hold. "I'll send the engineer on out, and I'll try to get out there tomorrow morning. Just keep things moving. If you have questions, call Eddie Mayfield."

13

THE END OF A CAMPAIGN

By the time Isadore arrived at my location, I could hear a siren wailing a few miles east on Highway 57. I guessed that a Mississippi patrolman had been alerted and was on the way to the scene. I gave my truck keys to the Peterson engineer and told him to head on to Leakesville and go over the plans with Dooley, then drive my truck back to his office in Maysville.

The colonel was obviously eager to get to the potential crime scene before too many conclusions could be drawn by Elrod and the state highway patrolman. We sped away in the Holt Security Company car, accelerating to a hundred miles an hour within a few seconds. Five minutes later, we turned onto a dirt road running through a pine forest. Blue lights were flashing in the distance.

I was pleased as hell to see a Black patrolman. Colonel Holt identified himself, and the patrolman appeared to be familiar with Isadore's company. I spoke from the passenger side. "Officer, I'm Delbert Cantrell, Cantrell Construction. I think that is one of my company trucks. Understand someone is inside. I have a pretty good idea who it might be. At least I know the man who is assigned the truck. He works for me."

"Well, Mr. Cantrell, the person in the truck doesn't work for anyone. There's not much left of him."

Elrod was busy taking notes and snapping pictures with a camera he got out of his patrol car. He stopped and came over to our car where Isadore and I were standing. "I don't think you want to look inside, Delbert—pretty gruesome. It's your truck for sure."

"It's mine all right, Elrod. I can see that."

"If there was any doubt, your company name is still visible on the right door. Was this Cecil's truck?"

"It was assigned to him. Guess he thought it was his."

Elrod wrote something down on his pad and went back to snapping pictures.

Colonel Holt moved over to the patrolman's vehicle. They talked out of my earshot, but I could hear bits and pieces of radio conversations between the patrolman and his dispatcher. It sounded as if he was having a difficult time explaining exactly where the burned vehicle was located. I barely heard Isadore offering some familiar landmarks. After a few minutes, he came back to his car.

He grinned. "The brother's down with it. He's called for a forensic detective. He's convinced it's a homicide, but for the moment, he has reported the cause as undetermined. The truck has probably been there for at least two days. I explained my association with you. Guess he saw some of the TV coverage concerning your arrest. He's got the real picture now."

"How long before the investigator gets here?"

"Probably two hours, coming from Hattiesburg. So, guess we're going to be here for a while. Meantime, the patrolman—Harris is his name—is calling for a meat wagon to come up from Pascagoula. They'll take the remains to the crime lab in Hattiesburg after the investigator is through here."

I felt as if I should look inside the truck but couldn't get past the odor of burned flesh hanging in the air. I had an urge to throw up and wondered how in the hell anyone could get close to the truck without heaving. I was trying to wrap my head around whatever in the hell was going on with Cecil Campbell. He had been such a dependable employee for ten years. And I knew one way or another, it was all tied to Carmen's murder. And I knew every authority involved would try to tie me to both crimes.

There are times in everyone's life when things seem to spin out of control. It happens even to the strongest among us. This was one of those moments for me. I sat in the colonel's car with the door open, waiting for a touch of nausea to pass. He came over and took a seat on the driver's side. We passed our ideas back and forth about what happened, agreeing that someone killed the man in the truck and set it on fire to destroy evidence.

"You know it wasn't accidental, Delbert," the colonel emphasized. "When you get close to the truck, in spite of other smells, there's an odor of gasoline still present."

"I just wonder who in the hell had it in for him besides me."

"Delbert, don't say that to anyone else. Loudermilk would love to get wind of it."

"Colonel, you know I had nothing to do with it. But I learned yesterday he had something going on with Carmen."

"My man, that woman got around, didn't she?"

"Like I said before, she was too beautiful for her own good."

My cell phone rang. I could see it was Sid Saperstein.

"Delbert, I just got a call from a friend who monitors the police calls. He says there's a burned-out Cantrell Construction truck near State Line with a body in it. Please tell me you don't know anything about that."

"Sorry, Sid, but I can't say that. I'm here now with Colonel Holt and the highway patrol. Elrod Jones is on the scene also."

"Listen, Delbert, don't make any statements. Don't talk to anyone. Whatever you might say will be wrong. That goddamn Loudermilk will be all over your ass on this one."

"I think it's out of Loudermilk's hands. The state has a forensic investigator on the way from Hattiesburg. Should be here in an hour or so."

"It's still in his jurisdiction, and I can't wait to see the headlines on this one. If you think you've been through the wringer, wait until this shit hits the fan: CUCKOLD HUSBAND KILLS WIFE AND LOVER."

"Do I need to come see you, Sid?"

"Yes, Delbert. Monday is too late. Tomorrow afternoon is filled, but we'll squeeze in a meeting tomorrow morning. I'll see you at ten. I have a court appearance but should be back by ten or so. We'll have lunch here."

"Yeah, Sid, we'll see you tomorrow."

I called to Elrod. He came around to the passenger side of Isadore's car. "Not much left of him, Delbert. The patrolman may want to ask you some questions. Just be careful what you say."

"Elrod, you don't think..."

"No, no, Delbert. It's just that you and I know we both can be hotheads. And this ain't the time for it."

"I just talked with Saperstein, and he advised me not to make a statement. Let Patrolman Harris know I'll turn over Cecil's personnel records from the office tomorrow. Beyond that, I have no idea what happened here, except that my truck and Cecil haven't been at my worksite in Leakesville since last Thursday."

"That takes care of our business here, Delbert. Guess I should wait a few more days before telling the sheriff I'm going to work for you."

"Yeah, Elrod, that might not look too good right now. Let's give it a week or so. I'll get one of the boarders to take care of things at the ranch until then." I thought of Vicky Metzger and her bootcut jeans.

Isadore and I got out of the car. He came around to my side. "You know, Delbert, I've come to respect you a lot in the short time we've known each other."

"That goes for me too."

"I've been thinking, trying to set some priorities in my life. Thank God I've got a wife with good practical sense. You know what she told me?"

"That would be hard to guess, Colonel."

"Well, she said I had better decide what is more important to me, satisfying my ego or taking care of the things I am responsible for."

"What did she mean by that?

"My running for the senate. She says that is just an ego trip."

"So what? A man is entitled to a little ego trip once in a while."

"No, Delbert, she's right. God, I've got three security contracts out of state with the government, guards at two local sites, a time-consuming job with you that now includes two murder investigations, and I want to see Sheriff Loudermilk defeated. My wife is carrying too much of the load."

"So, what are you going to do about it?"

"For one, I'm going to save you twenty-five thousand dollars."

"How's that?

"I'm dropping out of the senate race."

"Don't do that on my account, Isadore."

"No, and to be honest, it will make the state Republican Party mighty happy—bring back the Black vote to someone who can win, and I can devote time to getting Marge Wilson elected."

AN EMT CREW ARRIVED ABOUT AN HOUR LATER, AND we waited two hours more for the forensic investigator to arrive. He was an older gentleman, probably sixty- five, accompanied by a much younger lady detective. By then, it was approaching dusk and not much to see inside the truck without the handheld spotlight provided by the EMT crew.

The police officers all huddled together. After a few

minutes of conversation, the investigator asked Elrod to assist him in opening the driver's side door. But the intense heat from the fire had welded the door firmly shut. Elrod moved to the passenger door and pried it open with a tire tool he removed from the truck of his patrol car. I was irritated to see that the investigator spent no more than three or four minutes examining the body. *Hell,* I thought, *three hours waiting for you to get out here to confirm a piece of charcoal is not breathing. You're a cold little bastard. Not even a Hail Mary.*

He backed out of the truck, lifted his head, and spoke to no one in particular. "Not much I can do here. We need to get him back to the examination room. He looked in the direction of the patrol officer. "You guys got everything you need here?"

"Yes," the patrolman responded, then Elrod.

The investigator continued. "You definitely have a murder on your hands. It's obvious the fire was set, and I'm sure the victim didn't do that himself. The smell of gas is still intense inside the vehicle. We need to impound it until our investigation is complete. Can we get a tow truck out here?"

Elrod gave a half-hearted thumbs-up. "I've already called a tow company. He's on the way now. The truck will be held in the Cumbersome County compound in Maysville."

The EMT crew moved in with a black body bag. They opened it, then began pulling the burned corpse across the console and through the passenger door. As the bag was being zipped, I was struck by the unemotional way in which each person performed their job. I assumed they would have handled a burned log with the same dispassion. The finality of death struck me like a brick. I had plenty of reasons for not giving a damn about Cecil Campbell, but seeing what was left of him saddened me. *One minute, you're alive and breathing. The next minute you're gone as if you never existed.*

The lady detective spoke to Elrod and the highway patrolman. "You guys need anything more from us?"

No one responded.

"If not, we're on our way back to Hattiesburg."

Elrod and the patrolman shook her hand.

"I'll need copies of your reports." She handed each of them a business card. "My phone numbers and address. I would like to have everything in my hands by Monday, if possible."

The investigator added. "We'll be needing dental records. I guess that's a job for you, Deputy Jones, getting in touch with the deceased's probable next of kin and finding out which dentist might have those records. With them, we may be able to confirm his identity without waiting for DNA results." The EMTs loaded their cargo and spit dust and dirt back at us as their vehicle pulled away.

Isadore and I got into his car. He did a three-point turn. I lowered the window and called to Elrod. "Give me a call after you've spoken with Campbell's wife. He has a substantial insurance policy through my company that might interest her."

Isadore stepped on the gas, and we headed down the gravel road toward Highway 57.

14

THE FORENSIC REPORT

I was on my way from Leakesville to Saperstein's office when Elrod called. It was nearing 10 a.m., and my foot was heavy on the gas. One thing I had learned about Sid Saperstein, you didn't want to be late for a meeting with him. And that suited me fine. Nothing irritates me more than spending time twiddling my thumbs while I wait for someone to be where they are supposed to be.

"Delbert, I went to see Cecil's widow; Shirley's her name."

"Yeah, I know."

"I just wanted to tell you I went out there. It was strange. She didn't seem to be upset or surprised when I told her we found Cecil dead in his truck."

"Guess she was pissed at him. She probably knew about Carmen. You never know what is going on in someone's marriage." I chuckled at the thought crossing my mind. "Except in mine. Seems every damn body in the county, maybe the state, knows what was happening between Carmen and me."

"Another thing that struck me odd, she asked about an insurance policy with your company."

"Poor girl's all broken up, isn't she? What'd you tell her?"

"I told her I didn't know anything about it. She'd have to check with you."

"I'll let her know something when we get confirmation from the forensic lab."

"I told her you wouldn't know anything for at least a week or two, but she sure seemed awfully anxious about his insurance. Cold little bitch."

"Maybe she had her reasons. As I remember, she's a pretty good looker. Don't know why he would have fucked around on her. But who knows, she might have been hell to live with."

"She said last time she saw Cecil was a week ago when he got up to go to work."

"That must have been Thursday. Guess he made it to work, but according to Dooley, he must have changed his mind and left early."

"Well, Delbert, that sure leaves him without an alibi for the time Carmen was killed."

"Looks like he's not going to need an alibi, Elrod." It was with some satisfaction that I added, "Where he's gone, it wouldn't do him a hell of a lot of good. I don't think the man with the pitchfork gives two shits about an alibi."

"Anyway, Cecil's dentist is a guy by the name of Cheney in Pascagoula. I've already called his office and asked them to forward Cecil's records to Hattiesburg. They'll fax them up there today."

"Hey, man, I'm in a hurry, almost late for a meeting with my lawyer. You might want to take another crack at Shirley. I wouldn't be surprised if she knows more than she's saying."

"I'm plannin' on that."

"OK, let's talk later today or tomorrow when you get a chance."

"Yeah, buddy, catch you later."

COLONEL HOLT WAS SITTING IN HIS CAR, WAITING FOR me to arrive at Saperstein's office. Sid's car was not out front, so we assumed he was late getting out of court. Carolyn confirmed that when we got up to his office on the second floor. "Sid's on his way now; just left the courthouse. Go on into his office and make yourselves comfortable. Want some coffee?"

Isadore accepted. I turned it down.

While we waited, I brought the colonel up to date on Elrod's meeting with Shirley Campbell. He was as surprised as I was by her apparent lack of concern. "Maybe she's the type who keeps her feelings to herself, or maybe she had good reason for not caring. Nobody but her knows what was going on between them."

"You would still think the way he died might have prompted some reaction, but Elrod said she showed no emotion at all."

"Have you given much thought to who might have killed him?"

"I keep coming back to someone in the sheriff's

department, either Loudermilk or one of the deputies he's tight with."

"Harlan Haynes?"

"Nah, Harlan is dumb enough to do about anything Loudermilk asks except murder. He's not a bad guy, just a dumbass."

"How about that Vice boy?"

"Logan Vice? Now, there's a real possibility. And maybe his running mate, Stu McCarty, is just stupid enough to be dragged into it."

"By the way, I want to get out to the ranch this weekend and snoop around a little. One of the boarders might have noticed something we've missed. Anyone there I should stay away from?"

"I don't know most of them very well. That was Carmen's thing, not mine. But it might be interesting for you to talk with a gal by the name of Vicky Metzger. Cuts a damn nice figure in her western jeans, but I take her for a cold fish. She may tell you something she didn't want to share with me. You know how women are; they keep each other's secrets and lie when they have to."

"OK to let her know what I'm doing out there?"

"I think so. I'm calling her this afternoon and asking her to watch the ranch for me until I can get Elrod on the job. I'll let her know you're providing security for the place in the meantime."

"Who's next if she doesn't want to be helpful?

"You are, Colonel. Just go out there like you own the damn place."

"I've got something else in mind, a white dude who's

helped me before. If it's OK with you, I am going to put him on Logan Vice's tail. He works part time at a used car lot in Pascagoula, so he can drive a different car every day."

"That's fine with me if you think we can find something on Vice. I'd love to hang his arrogant ass."

WHEN SAPERSTEIN ARRIVED, HE TOOK CHARGE AS USUAL and began asking questions about the truck, the condition of the corpse, what law enforcement was on scene, and any statements I might have made to anyone out there.

I described the scene but left the description of the burned remains for Isadore.

"Did you make any statements that I should be aware of?"

"No," I said, not so emphatically.

"Nothing? Not to anyone? That doesn't sound like you, Delbert. I'm constantly going behind you to clean up your messes."

"Well, Counselor—I think Sid liked to be called Counselor—this time, there's nothing to clean up. I promise"

"Name, rank, and serial number." Sid smiled just a little. "That's what they teach you in the army, and that's what I try to teach my clients, but damn, Delbert, you are a tough case."

Isadore came to my rescue. "There's no problem this time, Mr. Saperstein. The only thing Delbert told the patrolman was his name and that the truck was his."

"You should have stopped with your name, Delbert. Let him figure out who owned the truck."

"Hell, man, my name is still on the door of the truck."

"But you get the picture, don't you? Those bastards can twist anything you say. My advice to any client is to say nothing without a lawyer present."

"I have nothing to hide."

"You think so?"

"Don't you, Sid?"

"Sure, but that isn't what anyone who looks at your situation objectively might think. It's usually the husband. As I told you, Delbert, someone murdered your wife and her lover. And you, sir, are the number one suspect until we find the killer or killers."

Isadore broke in. "Delbert didn't talk to anyone but Elrod Jones. I spoke with the highway patrolman, just rapping a little with a brother." He chuckled.

"You be careful, Delbert, what you say to anyone, including Elrod. He's still in a deputy uniform and still reports to Sheriff Loudermilk. That can spell trouble for you if Elrod inadvertently divulges something you might have said. On the other hand, it can be bad for Elrod if he withholds facts or evidence."

I could see the concern on Isadore's face. "I thought we were getting a handle on Carmen's murder, but this Campbell thing has sure added new complications. I'm not sure where we begin. How about you, Delbert?"

"Like you said, Colonel, you need to spend some time at the ranch, and I think it's a good idea to put a tail on Deputy Vice. Elrod will be working on Campbell's widow to see if she knows anything. I'll be spending some time to manage a campaign to elect a new sheriff."

"How's that coming?" Sid asked.

"OK, I think. We have a full-page ad running Sunday and a half-page every week for the next six weeks. Our radio ads start today on six stations, four times an hour. TV ads will run in the evening on three stations every hour. We've paid for time for Marge Wilson to be on all three local stations once each week. She will explain why she's running and show the viewers how to fill in her name on the ballot. The colonel has decided to drop out of his state senate race to devote more time to Marge Wilson's campaign in his spare time."

"I told you I would help. What do you want from me?"

"Tell you what, Sid, I think about a hundred K is about right."

"Delbert, since my net worth is about 10 percent of yours, I think twenty thousand is about right since you're spending two hundred thousand."

"Or more. You have as much interest in getting rid of Loudermilk, Counselor, so how about making it twenty-five?"

"Twenty, Delbert, twenty."

"Thanks, Sid, that's really more than I anticipated."

Isadore erupted with laughter. "You millionaires arguing over pennies."

I turned to him. "Speaking of millionaires, I would think you're not far from that, my man. If not now, you will be when you finish billing me."

We all laughed.

Sid resumed in a serious mood. "Our DNA evidence is being expedited, and we should have preliminary results in about two weeks. Like you, I expect the blood will be confirmed as Carmen's. If we're lucky, we'll have a second party's DNA from the coffee cup. Let's hope it doesn't match Cecil Campbell."

"Why is that?" I asked.

The colonel answered. "If it is Campbell's, it might strengthen the sheriff's expected argument that you murdered both of them. If it belongs to another party, we may have a candidate of our own for killing them."

Sid nodded. "Now you know why I recommended this guy to you, Delbert."

I shook my head. "Gents, let me give you a little bit of advice: Don't ever fall for a sweet-talking southern beauty who can tell you a lie without batting an eye. You see the mess it can get you into."

Sid's serious face returned. "I'm happy that you can find humor in your situation. But this may be more of a problem than you realize, Delbert."

"I don't think so, Sid. I know I'm in deep shit."

THAT AFTERNOON, I CALLED GULF COAST ADVERTISING to confirm the schedule for Marge's taped commercials and to set up her live interviews with the local television channels. Afterward, I got Marge on the phone to see how she was handling Sheriff Loudermilk. "Sweet as pie," she said but did admit she had taken some ribbing from her fellow deputies. We made plans to get together at her house on Monday evening for dinner. I was hoping she might serve more of her great meatloaf.

After Marge, I called Vicky Metzger and arranged for her to deal with all our boarders until I could get a manager on site. I let her know Isadore would be spending time at the ranch and might want to ask her some questions. She promised to be cooperative "if there is anything I can add to what I've already told you." Frankly, I was a little worried about that relationship but hoped it could endure the two weeks until Elrod would be there full time. Of course, that depended on how smoothly the investigation of Campbell's presumed death progressed.

On Saturday morning, I awoke full of piss and vinegar. I soon eliminated the piss but retained the vinegar. I had some things on my mind I needed to talk about with Eddie Mayfield, so I drove out to my equipment compound where I knew I would find Eddie on the job. He was the most dependable man I had, much like me—smart and energetic, honest and trustworthy. He was eager to show me his new truck—the one I paid for.

"I took the old one up to Dooley."

I gave him a disdainful look.

He smiled, "Hell, Boss, it isn't that old—maybe two years and low mileage. He'll get another two hundred thousand miles out of that truck."

"And what will you get out of that machine?" I pointed to the pristine white Ford Off-Road F-250.

"At least that much, I would say."

I slapped him on the shoulder. "It's all right, Eddie. I guess our vice president deserves a new truck, don't you?"

"What do you mean?"

"Come on. I'll show you."

We walked upstairs to my office. I opened the door, holding it ajar, and gestured with my open hand. "Come on into your office, Mr. Vice President."

"You're shitting me, Boss."

"No, Eddie, you're going to have to take up a lot of slack. I have too many problems on my plate right now, and you're the best man I have. I'm relying on you to run the operation just the way I would. I'll be working out of my home office and hope to be available any time you need me."

He grabbed my hand and shook it, grinning like a kid, belying thirty-five years of age. "You won't be sorry, Delbert. I promise."

I looked at him sternly. "I'd better not be."

"When do I start?"

"Now." I said, "And I'll get my personal things out of your office next week. Also, your secretary will have to work for me too for a while—nothing she can't handle over the phone or computer. We'll see how that works."

"I'm ready, Delbert."

"And by the way, your pay will increase to something appropriate."

"Thanks. Okay if I call my wife and tell her?"

"Yes, then let's give that truck of yours a workout on the way to Leakesville. Dooley is waiting for us there."

Fifteen minutes later, we were on our way upstate to our worksite. Eddie pushed the truck to eighty. I sat back and thought about all the events taking place in my life. At least I had managed to make one person happy, and he was sitting tall behind the wheel of the Cantrell flying machine.

The phone rang. It was Elrod.

"Delbert, you're not supposed to know this yet."

"Know what?"

"I just got a call from Hattiesburg. They've compared the dental chart to the burned corpse. It isn't Campbell."

"Who the hell is it then?"

"We don't know."

15

GOOD NEWS

"Pull over," I instructed Eddie as I dialed Saperstein's home phone number.

His wife answered. "Saperstein residence."

"Mrs. Saperstein, this is Delbert Cantrell. I need to speak with Sid."

"I'm sorry, Mr. Cantrell, he's golfing and doesn't wish to be called."

"Thank you, ma'am. I understand. Let him know I called when he gets home. It's rather urgent." But I knew before she said goodbye I wasn't waiting for Sid to get off the golf course.

I dialed his cell phone and waited. After four rings he answered. "This better be an emergency, Delbert. I'm putting for a birdie."

"Get ready for a hole-in-one."

"Yeah, what is it?"

"Cecil Campbell. It wasn't him in the truck."

There was silence for seconds before Sid answered in a measured voice. "How do you know that?"

"Dental records don't match."

"Holy shit."

"Yeah, no wonder his little wife wasn't too upset when Elrod broke the news to her. She probably knew it wasn't Cecil."

"Yes, I would say she knows what's going on. And this complicates the hell out of our investigation. It will bring in the MBI and FBI for sure in order to find Campbell."

"And find out who was burned in the truck."

"Well, Delbert I need to putt before we hold up the next foursome. Let me give some thought to this, and I will call you later today. And I caution you, if the press comes after you, you have nothing to say on the advice of your attorney."

"That ought to set the rumor mill into motion big time."

"Probably, but we sure as hell don't want to provide grist for that mill."

"I get you, Counselor. I'm on my way to Leakesville now, but will be home later today. We can talk then. I'll call Colonel Holt and let him know what we've learned."

"Delbert, just one thing more you may not have considered. This is good news for you."

"How's that?"

"At least you won't be a suspect in Campbell's death, and he will be the suspect for the corpse found in his truck."

"My goddamn truck, Sid. It was my truck Campbell set on fire, not his. Maybe I'm not a suspect in his death now, but I damn well will be if I find that son of a bitch before the authorities do."

"Careful who you say that to, Delbert. It may come back to bite you in the ass."

"Tell me something, Sydney—I knew he hated to be called Sydney—why do you always tell me you have to attend Temple on Saturday when I invite you to golf with me? It wouldn't have anything to do with the fact that I'm a twenty handicap, would it?"

He cleared his throat, his impatience coming right through the phone. "You don't want me to win any more of your money on the golf course, do you? Besides, this is strictly business, Delbert. Even God understands that."

"Since I have no desire to argue with God, the least I can do is to wish you good luck with that birdie."

WE GOT BACK ON THE ROAD. MY NEXT CALL WAS TO Colonel Holt. He was at the ranch and had cornered our Miss Vickie Metzger. I heard him tell her he might want to speak with her again. Then he turned his attention to the news I had just given him.

"Delbert, that makes the DNA from that coffee cup all the more important. I'll lay you ten to one it's Campbell's."

"Who knows, Colonel? Could be anyone's. It might belong to one of the boarders who just stopped in to shoot the shit. It will be a stroke of luck if it matches the person in the truck."

"When we get right down to it, if it isn't his DNA, we'll be looking for a needle in a haystack unless it happens to match someone in the national database."

"But we might be able to eliminate a couple of people if

we can get samples. That would include Campbell and half the sheriff's department."

"Don't forget yourself."

"Believe me, I haven't forgotten. And I know the only thing that will clear me is to find her killer."

"I'm working on it, Delbert. I'm working on it."

"By the way, how are things going with Miss Vicky?"

"Finest kind," he said. "She's talking up a storm, knows a lot of dudes in and out of here. Maybe you know all of them, maybe not."

"Who, for example?"

"Gerald Hinson, our friend Deputy Vice, the sheriff himself."

"I get the picture."

"She's still filling me in.'"

"Don't get distracted by that cute little ass."

"No, not a worry here, my friend. I have way too much at risk for something like that. Mrs. Holt is a very jealous woman." He laughed. "Greedy too, and don't you ever tell her I said that."

"I've got you covered, Colonel."

"When do you want to get together again?"

"Let's see how things go. I'm on my way to my jobsite. I'll be back home late this afternoon if you need me. Unless someone else comes up missing, I am sitting on my ass the rest of the day and tomorrow. I need a breather."

"Going to count your money?"

"Yeah, I want to make sure I've got enough to pay your bill."

"All right, Delbert, guess we can wait until Monday to talk again."

"Yeah, but be sure to catch Marge's TV appearances this evening, and let me know what you think about our candidate. She has taped interviews on all three channels."

EDDIE AND I SPENT THE AFTERNOON GOING OVER PLANS and schedules with Dooley. I was impressed with the way he had taken charge of the project, and I could see from the interaction of Dooley and Eddie that I had a good team going forward. All foundations and footings for the strip mall buildings were in place. We took inventory of the materials required for the next phase of construction, making certain everything was on hand or scheduled for just-in-time delivery. The three of us capped our day with beer and pizza at *Pronto Pizza and Subs* before heading back to Maysville.

I arrived home in time to shower before sitting down with a second beer to watch Marge in her taped television debut. She stood at a podium, probably elevated, appearing almost as tall as the lanky Elrod Jones who stood by her. Dressed in her deputy's uniform and flanked by the American flag to her right and the Mississippi state flag to her left, she introduced herself to the citizens of Cumbersome County.

"Hello, I am Deputy Marge Wilson of the Cumbersome County Sheriff's Department, where I have served for the past three years. I am now running for sheriff. I want to explain to all of you my reasons for offering myself as a candidate for that office. I am not doing it out of a sense of entitlement as Sheriff Loudermilk does every four years. He believes the office belongs to him. I am not doing it in order to enrich myself, as Sheriff Loudermilk and Deputy Harlan Haynes will do. I am running in order to ensure that our laws are enforced justly and fairly for all citizens regardless of income, political influence, race, gender, religion, or creed. I am running to ensure that all citizens of Cumbersome County will feel secure in their homes and can trust our law enforcement officers to be honest custodians of our security and safety.

"Under my direction, no unnecessary funds will be spent to repaint department vehicles to suit my personal whims as Sheriff Loudermilk has done with each new election. No funds will be spent unnecessarily to decorate my office, as Sheriff Loudermilk has done over and over. No funds will be pilfered for personal use, as Sheriff Loudermilk and Deputy Haynes have been accused of doing. No kickbacks will be tolerated as Sheriff Loudermilk has been accused of tolerating and accepting.

"Under my administration, new hiring practices will be enforced. You will note that in a county of nearly eighty thousand people, 25 percent of whom are Black, there are no Black officials in the sheriff's department. You will note that in that same county of eighty thousand people, 50 percent of whom are women, I am the only female in the sheriff's department. Let me promise you this: I will not replace any current deputy unless it is warranted, and I will not hire any new deputies or office personnel unless absolutely needed. But when new positions are filled, everyone, regardless of gender or race will be fairly considered for every position. There will be no racial preference. Only the best candidates, regardless of gender or race, will be hired."

Marge turned her attention to a sample ballot projected

on a screen. She pointed toward the blank spaces beneath Sheriff Loudermilk and Deputy Harlan Haynes. "Note that my name is not on this ballot. And because of time limitations, it will not appear on the ballot when you step into the booth to vote. But you can vote for me by writing in my name, Marge Wilson or M. Wilson. That is all there is to it. Be sure to spell my name correctly M-a-r-g-e W-i-l-s-o-n, or just M. Wilson.

"For those of you who don't know me, I am fifty-two years old. I have an associate degree from Gulf Coast Junior College in Law Administration. I was born in Pascagoula but have lived most of my life in Maysville with my husband, Ralph. We have two grown daughters who live with their families in Cumbersome County near Leakesville. I am running for sheriff for them and every other family in our county.

"My ads will continue on this station and other local stations. They will run in the *Town Crier* every day until the election. If you check the paper, you will see a sample ballot with my name written in, just the way you should do it on voting day, November 4th."

"You're all right, girl," I said to the television. "You just won my vote and more than half of this county."

16

A WOUNDED PREY

I did my best to relax on Sunday, but by mid-afternoon, the intensity of my anger got the best of me, and I had to get on the road before I exploded. Cecil Campbell plagued my mind, and I couldn't move on to anything else. So, I decided to give his wife, Shirley, a call to do a little investigating of my own. I was convinced she was involved with him in a scheme to defraud me and my insurance company, but I wanted proof. I was certain no one was dumb enough to let her know about the mismatch with Cecil's dental records. I would blindside her if I could talk with her before she learned about them.

"Hi, Shirley, Delbert Cantrell here."

"Yes, Mr. Cantrell, how are you?"

"I'm well in spite of all that has happened recently. But I know you have been through quite a bit also."

"Yes," she said. "It hasn't been easy.

"I haven't had a chance to speak with you about Cecil. I know this has all been a terrible shock, and I would like to do what I can to help. You know there are some insurance matters and salary that will go to you. Is it possible for me to stop by in about an hour to discuss these things with you?"

"I'm really not feeling very well today," she said, giving me concerns that she might be suspicious of my call. That concern made my meeting with her all the more urgent.

"I would like to wait until tomorrow, but my schedule is awfully tight. This afternoon is the only chance I will have to see you until next weekend." I was careful not to bring up the subject of dental records. "You know it may be several weeks for DNA test results on Cecil's remains, and I don't want you to wait that long for some financial assistance from the company. I need to talk with you before I decide how to handle any claims you might have."

"As I said, I am not feeling very well, but if you think it's necessary, we can meet this afternoon for a little while."

"All right, Shirley. I will see you in about an hour."

After shaving and freshening up, I made the twenty-minute trip across town. The Campbell residence was a three-bedroom bungalow sitting on five acres of land, on which Cecil always planted a garden in the spring. But this time of year, the garden spot was covered with brown corn stalks and other dead growth, obvious evidence that summer had come and gone. A brown and black spotted hound, ears flopping over the sides of its head, came from under the house and barked. Two other mutts, slightly smaller but just as loud, rounded the house. The three of them set up a chorus, yapping as they encircled me. After a stern scolding and then a few kind words, they all wagged their tails and sauntered alongside me as I stepped onto the porch.

A curtain at the front window fluttered. I heard footsteps

approaching just as I placed my finger on the doorbell. Before it could ring, the door opened, and Shirley, appearing tired and older than I recalled, stood facing me. The attractive young woman who had attended several company events with her husband was gone. She opened the door further and stepped back, waiting for me to enter.

"Good to see you again," I said. "I'm sorry it's under these circumstances."

If she was happy to see me, she was able to conceal her feelings. "Come in, Mr. Cantrell." She motioned toward a recliner, and I sat down.

Hours of Your Lives or something similar, was on the TV. Apparently, she didn't want to miss the episode because she turned down the volume but did not mute the sound. All the while we talked, the television moaned and groaned in the background. It was the kind of sappy dialogue that made my back teeth hurt. I couldn't help but think, *damn, if you want to feel like hell, just watch and listen to this shit.*

She took a seat across from me, a long blond coffee table separating us. I tried to start what I anticipated would be an awkward conversation, but she spoke before I could. "Mr. Cantrell, don't think I'm hard-hearted, but I would like to know something about the life insurance policy your company provided for Cecil."

Still in mourning, I thought. "Sure, Mrs. Campbell, that's one of the things I want to talk to you about. Also, your health insurance with the company, you know, how long it will continue and so forth."

"OK. And you mentioned something about some pay that is due to Cecil now. When will I get that?"

"Well, I want to go over everything with you, but I need to get some information first."

She abruptly stood, putting her forefinger to her lips as if to make certain I didn't speak. I watched and listened as she turned up the volume. Animated and smiling, she pointed to the TV screen. "That's Charles," she said. "They just found his long-lost twin brother—well, he really isn't his brother, but an impostor—in a jungle in Cambodia. And he doesn't know that somebody knows he killed the real brother. You know what I mean. And would you believe it? He's now the mayor of a Cambodian village or something. And the people in the show are just now learning some details."

"Do you want me to come back later? Or we can wait while you watch the rest of this show if you would like."

"No. I guess it isn't that important to you." Scowling, she lowered the volume and took her seat again.

"It's all right," I said. "I understand how it could be important to you."

"No, I'm sorry I interrupted you, but I had seen most of that episode and didn't want to miss the part about Charles's brother—his supposed brother ... you know what I mean. I already missed that part last week when it first played."

It was a difficult task to act as if her actions were perfectly normal, but I tried. We sat in silence for several seconds simply looking at each other. She appeared small and pale, as if she had shrunk to half her size as she sank back into her chair. Whatever was going on in her life was taking an obvious toll, and I was dealing with a wounded prey. The title of a Jane Fonda movie, *They Shoot Horses Don't They*, meandered through my brain, and I thought about how pathetic it would be to destroy her. But regardless of my empathy, I was determined to learn what part she played in Cecil's scheme. That realization brought me back to the reason I was now sitting across from Shirley Campbell.

"When did you last see Cecil?"

I think the abruptness of my question set her back on her heels, and she took a moment to answer. "Let me think, last Saturday or Sunday, I believe."

But according to Elrod, Shirley had last seen her husband on Thursday, the morning he left for work, the morning before Carmen was murdered.

"Are you sure?" The sound of my voice told her I knew she was lying.

"Let me think."

"Yeah, make certain you get it right. It's important."

"Now that I think about it, it was Sunday afternoon when I saw him."

"A week ago?"

"Yes, Sunday."

"You know he wasn't at work on Friday, don't you?"

"I wouldn't have any way of knowing that, Mr. Cantrell."

"Did he come home Thursday night or Friday?"

"No. When he left for work on Thursday, I didn't see him again until Sunday."

"Wasn't that out of the ordinary? I mean, for him to be gone for three days and nights without you knowing his whereabouts?"

"No, it wasn't. Cecil often didn't come home from work at night."

"Didn't you wonder where he was?"

"There was no wondering. I knew he was with that bitch."

I didn't have to ask but did anyway. "What bitch?"

Color returned to her face, and she appeared invigorated by the anger she expressed. "That whore, the one who was murdered last week, your wife, Mr. Cantrell. You know who I'm talking about."

"My estranged wife," I clarified. "I didn't know they were involved. How much did you know?"

"I knew for a while, but on Thursday morning, he told me they were in love, and he wanted a divorce. But when he came home Sunday, he had changed his mind. He asked me to forgive him."

"Was everything all right between you then?"

"I thought so, but after he ate lunch and read the Sunday paper, he said he had to go see someone."

"Something you just said bothers me."

"What?"

"Why did you tell Deputy Jones you had not seen Cecil since Thursday morning?"

"Because I didn't want to answer a lot of questions about Cecil, and if you don't mind, Mr. Cantrell, I'm getting tired. I really don't want to answer any more of yours."

"Let me just ask you one more question."

"What's that?"

"Are you mixed up in Carmen's death or the corpse that burned in my truck out on Highway 57?"

She stood, looking down at me. If she was not insulted, she was doing a damn good job of pretending. "Don't be ridiculous. Why would I have anything to do with that? It was my husband in the truck."

She took two or three steps toward the front door. I followed, talking to the back of her head. "About the corpse— are you sure it was Cecil?"

She stopped and turned to look at me, her anger gone, her face awash with innocence. "It was my husband. You said so yourself."

"No, honey, I didn't. But I know it isn't Cecil."

"Now you're really being ridiculous. You told me it would be several weeks before there were any DNA results. How do you know it's not him?"

"We have his dental records, and they don't match the corpse."

Her eyes widened. "If it isn't Cecil, who else could it be?"

"I don't know, but I think you do."

She appeared pained and speechless, obviously searching for a believable explanation.

"Shirley, you want to sit again and talk about it? I think you are in a real legal mess."

She dropped into the nearest seat and put her hands to her face. "I told Cecil we would get into a lot of trouble, but he said it was the only way out. He was involved in something with one of the sheriff's deputies. I don't know what it was, but it had something to do with stealing materials from your company. He had a drug habit— OxyContin—concealed it from everyone somehow, that is, everyone but me."

I remained standing, looking down at her, sensing that I had her where I wanted. "He sure as hell concealed it from me—that and a lot of other things. But how about the corpse in my truck? Who is he?"

"I don't know, Mr. Cantrell. Honest."

"Is it someone Cecil killed?"

"I don't know for sure, but it might be."

I knew the answer to my next question but wanted to hear her explanation. "Why would he kill somebody and burn them in my truck?"

"He said he had to disappear."

"And he wanted to fake his own death. Is that what happened?"

"I guess."

"Where would he disappear to?"

"Maybe Mexico or Canada. He said he would get in touch with me when he was safe. He said I could collect his insurance, and the boys and I could get by for two or three years while he was getting things straight." She burst into tears. "I knew this was going to happen, but he wouldn't listen to me."

I took hold of her hand. "I'm sorry, Shirley."

"How much trouble am I in?"

"A lot, but I'll try to help you if you will be completely honest with me."

"I will. I swear."

"For starters, was anyone with Cecil when he showed up here last Sunday? Someone gave him a ride after he set my truck on fire?"

"No, he was alone, driving the company truck. He said he was tired and wanted to take a nap. But after he read the newspaper, he left. Said he had to go see someone."

"And you're telling me that was the last time you saw him."

"Yes."

"Why are you still trying to protect Cecil?"

"What do you mean?"

"You know a hell of a lot more than you're telling me. But if you would rather tell the police, that's OK with me."

"What do you think I haven't told you?"

"The truth about the last time you saw Cecil. When was that? It had to be after a man was killed and my truck set afire."

She burst into tears again. "It was Wednesday—Wednesday morning. He came home and told me he had to leave, and he was in a lot of trouble."

"Was he by himself?"

"No, he came with some guy. They didn't stay long."

"You never heard his name?"

"No, Cecil called him GG, I think. When we were in the kitchen alone, Cecil said he was just a friend—someone he had a beer with occasionally."

"What did he look like?"

"Tall and scruffy, wore cowboy boots and jeans, loud-talking, a real rough-looking guy."

"Gerald Hinson. You ever heard that name?"

"I don't think so."

"Bad teeth?"

"Yes," she said. "Brown, like heavy smoking or chewing tobacco."

"Probably Hinson."

"Am I in trouble, Mr. Cantrell?"

I thought, *hell yes,* but said, "Not yet. It's a good thing you didn't file false insurance claims. You would have made yourself complicit in murder as well as insurance fraud. As far as I'm concerned, everything you've told me is strictly between us." Who was I going to tell besides my lawyer? I sure as hell couldn't trust anyone else.

"Thank you. I really appreciate your help. It's good to get this off my conscience."

I got up to leave. "I'll be in touch with you."

"Before you go, can you tell me about Cecil's back pay? I really need it."

I took out my wallet and handed her five one-hundred-dollar bills. "He has more than this coming. I'll check tomorrow and let you know. By the way, Cecil has a large 401K savings that you may be able to access. I'll let you know about that, too." I needed to keep Shirley working with me, and if it took a few hundred dollars to make sure, that suited me just fine.

"How about health insurance? Is that still effective? I need it for the boys."

Damn, I thought. *You know how to press an advantage.* "Yes, I'll carry that for you for at least six months."

She opened the door, stood on her toes, and kissed my cheek. "Thank you, Mr. Cantrell. I'm sorry Cecil did you so wrong."

"He didn't treat you so well either."

It occurred to me that Mrs. Campbell could be clever when she needed to be. In spite of her wounds, she had emerged from our encounter, at least even with me. But I told myself, *it's only round one, and we're coming out swinging at the bell.* I got into my truck and backed out of the driveway, happy not to have lost my britches.

I turned my truck for home, took out my cell phone, and dialed the colonel.

"No rest for the weary. Don't you know it's Sunday, Delbert?"

"Yes, Colonel, but all the days are the same to me. I have a little task I would like for you to do."

"What is it, and can it wait until tomorrow?"

"The answer to the second question is yes. The answer to the first is a little more complicated."

"I'm listening."

"I want you to find out everything you can about a redneck asshole by the name of Gerald Hinson. Where does he live and work? Is he still married or shacking up? Is he alive? I'll tell you more about him and Cecil Campbell when we meet tomorrow. We need to find Campbell, too. You won't mind taking your wife to Mexico on my dime, would you?"

"Keep talking, Delbert."

"Tomorrow, Colonel. Tomorrow, I'll tell you all about it."

17

A WEDDING IN THE WORKS

I drove home with a feeling that Shirley Campbell was in a quandary, not of her choosing, but one that could very easily get worse if she continued to protect her husband. I had strong doubts she had told me all she knew about Cecil's whereabouts. It would be interesting to read her comments to the sheriff in the *Town Crier*, because, almost certainly, he would be hunting for a headline in the newspaper and a chance to get on television. News about the unidentified corpse found in my truck would be fodder for every news venue in the state of Mississippi, and Loudermilk would ride the crest as frequently and as long as possible. Mrs. Campbell would undoubtedly be the center of the sheriff's attention while the crest lasted.

As I expected, the Sunday evening news lead story was about the unidentified corpse and missing suspect, Cecil Campbell, employee of Cantrell Construction, Maysville, Mississippi. The report carried a video of a charred white truck being hooked to the tow vehicle. The camera zoomed in to show the distorted name of Cantrell Construction on the passenger door. Luckily, the meat wagon had already left the scene, preventing reporters from showing the gruesome details of the blackened remains of the unknown victim.

"...Mr. Campbell was a key employee of Mr. Delbert Cantrell, who was arrested recently for the murder of his estranged wife, Carmen Cantrell. Even though he was released for insufficient evidence in that murder, Mr. Cantrell still remains a suspect according to Cumberland County Sheriff John Loudermilk. Unconfirmed reports of a relationship between Mrs. Cantrell and Mr. Campbell raise serious new questions which Mr. Cantrell will, no doubt, be expected to answer."

"You empty-headed bitch." I aimed my venom at a cookie-cutter journalist, all of twenty-five years old and full of journalism school wisdom and idealistic bullshit. I should have saved the diatribe running in my head for the sheriff, who now had his hands wrapped around a microphone.

"Yes, we will be askin' Mr. Cantrell to come in to answer some questions. But let me make clear that, as of now, we have no reason to believe he was involved in this new development. I have a crack team of deputies, headed by Deputy Elrod Jones, lookin' into this matter. We will be cooperatin' with the Mississippi Bureau of Investigation and the federal authorities. You can be sure that I will stay personally involved until both crimes are solved."

I began with, *you dumb fucking fat-bellied son of a bitch,* and I intended to add a few more choice names. Before I could continue, my house phone rang. It was Sydney Saperstein.

"Delbert, are you watching the news?"

"I was until that fat bastard began running his lip. I just turned off the TV to keep me from throwing a brick through the goddamn screen."

"Well, Delbert, I don't give a damn what you do to your TV. I just wanted to tell you that you will not make a statement. You will not answer any questions. You will refer that fat bastard, as you call him to your lawyer."

"Saperstein, you know damn well I have no intention of telling Loudermilk anything except to get fucked."

"Not even that. Let him talk to your lawyer."

"Sydney, I would really be touched if I thought you cared about me. But I think you're just trying to pad your fee. Besides, I don't think you'll tell John Loudermilk to get fucked."

"Goodbye, Delbert. And don't call me Sydney."

"What time are we getting together tomorrow?"

"In the afternoon. I'll call you in the morning."

"Thanks."

"You're welcome."

"Goodbye, Sydney."

THE NEXT MORNING, EDDIE MAYFIELD AND I DROVE TO Mobile to meet with Army Corps of Engineers reps to discuss a bid proposal we submitted for construction of a waterfront facility in Eufaula, Alabama. About ten-thirty, I dropped off Eddie at our equipment compound then went to meet with Colonel Holt at the closest Waffle House for a quick brunch.

The colonel had already done some digging on Gerald

Hinson: his arrests, convictions, and other public information available on the internet. He had also obtained a record of Hinson's string of addresses up to a year or so ago. Among his arrests were charges of spousal battery, petty theft, and repeat DUIs. There was one charge that raised both the colonel's and my eyebrows—arson of a car repair shop.

Colonel Holt laid out his plans for finding Hinson. "The first thing I want to do is to locate his ex-wife and any girlfriends who might have heard from him."

"I don't think he'll go too far. He needs to be here for a hearing for his latest DUI and suspended driver's license. That should be coming up soon. You can probably find out when it's scheduled by checking at the clerk's office downtown. He should have a bond posted, which means the bail bondsman will also have an interest in his whereabouts."

"I'll get a handle on that and check to see if Ballard's Bail Bonds is hung out on this one."

"Shit, I hope so. Old Sam Ballard will be out there himself looking for the son of a bitch if he thinks Hinson's trying to jump bail. Could save us a whole lot of time and trouble."

Our food came, and we began to eat. The colonel downed two eggs, sausage, and hash browns with a waffle on the side while I ate a burger and bowl of chili. Neither of us attempted to carry on a deep conversation as we stuffed our faces.

My phone rang. Saperstein let me know he would see me at 2 p.m. "Will the colonel be with you?"

"No, I'll be giving him the lowdown on Shirley Campbell as soon as I finish this bowl of chili. It's the same thing I will tell you this afternoon. The colonel has other concerns right now, the main one, a punk by the name of Gerald Hinson."

"OK, see you at two."

I filled the colonel in on what I did and didn't learn from Shirley Campbell. He agreed she probably wasn't telling me all she knew, and I assured him I wasn't through dealing with her.

"But, Colonel, there's someone else that bothers me in more ways than one."

"Who's that?"

"Vicky Metzger. The cut of her jeans sure piques my interest, but there's something about her that keeps me wondering if she's also hiding something."

"Well, Delbert, you may have good cause for your suspicions. I had a feeling she was holding out too. It seems to me she spent too much time at the ranch not to know everything that went on. I've already made up my mind to have another run at her when the time is right."

We finished our lunch and went our separate ways, the colonel to the Maysville courthouse and me to see Saperstein.

Fifteen minutes into my trip, my younger brother, Keith, called from Dallas. "Hey, brother, you're making the news way out here in Texas. I see you killed that blonde bombshell you were married to."

He laughed until I said, "Little brother, I'll be laughing my ass off when something like this happens to you."

"Don't worry, Del, it ain't going to ever happen to me."

"Don't be too sure, punk. I've seen some of those babes hanging onto your arm. One of these days, you'll end up with one just like Carmen. And she'll take you for every dime you've got."

"Like I said, it isn't ever going to happen to me."

"All right, stud. Did you call to razz me or can I do something for you?" I often dropped a few thousand dollars Keith's way even when he didn't ask for it.

"No, I just called to let you know I love you and to invite you to my wedding."

"I thought you were never getting married."

"I didn't say that."

"Who's the lucky girl?"

"Lucky boy, Delbert."

He must have heard my silence as I tried to comprehend what I had just been told.

"Did you hear me, Del? Lucky boy. Benny Sanford and I are getting married, and you're invited."

"Damn," I said.

"You know Benny. His parents own the Sanford Department Stores chain."

"Hell, brother, I didn't know you were queer."

"Neither did I."

"At least you're marrying well."

He laughed, but I heard a little self-deprecation in his chuckle. "Looks as if he's the one who should be worried about being taken for everything he has... I sure don't have anything for him to take."

I said the only thing I thought was appropriate. "I love you, brother."

"Will you come?"

"I'm awfully busy here; not sure at all about future plans."

"Will you come be my best man, brother?"

"Damn, Keith, that's mighty hard to wrap my head around right now."

"It won't happen until January. You can make up your mind before that. But it will mean the world to me if you'll come."

"Give me a few days to think about it."

"I will, Delbert. Take your time."

"I'll let you know."

"I know I can depend on you being here."

By the time I hung up the phone, I also knew. He was my brother, and I would be there by his side. I called him back five minutes later and told him so.

I WAS STILL WRESTLING WITH MY BROTHER'S revelation when I pulled my truck into a parking space in front of Saperstein's office. The meeting went as I expected with Sid reemphasizing the rules of the legal game we were embroiled in, a game that was getting more complicated by the day. He didn't have to waste a lot of time on the subject but made certain I understood the seriousness of my situation. For some strange reason, Sid was under the impression I might blow my stack at a most inappropriate time and end up with a nightstick alongside my head once again. For the life of me, I couldn't guess where he got such an idea.

I told him about my visit with Shirley Campbell. "I think she's still protecting that bastard even after he's used her every way possible. And we can expect another shoe to drop when the sheriff starts going after her. Thankfully, Elrod Jones is heading the investigation for Loudermilk, and if anything goes down with that, he'll certainly let me know."

"That might be a problem for us, or Elrod might turn up something that helps. It worries me that we are sitting on possible evidence that should be turned over to the authorities. Until now, our only concern was our dipshit sheriff. But now that the state and the feds are getting involved, we have to be careful about concealing or withholding evidence. My position now is that we are not sure it is evidence, and we won't know for certain until the lab results come back."

"Do you think the lab will let anyone know they are performing DNA for us?"

"I've been assured by Dr., Schmidt that he won't volunteer anything. But you know, if he is asked, he will have to reveal that information."

"The colonel and I are working our end of the problem. He's trying to get a handle on Gerald Hinson and learn what he can about Cecil Campbell. That may require a trip to the border or even into Mexico if it appears that's where he fled."

"Ok, Delbert. Let's see if we can get a handle on things by the time the DNA results come in. I hope that will be a week from Friday. Unless something else happens, we probably won't need to talk again until then."

My cell phone rang. It was Elrod Jones. "We need to talk, Delbert, just you and me. Can I meet you at your place?"

"Sure. I'll be home in about half an hour."

I shook hands with Sydney. "Let me know if anything changes."

"Are you holding out on me? Who was on the phone?"

"Of course not, Sid. It was my gardener." I couldn't explain, even to myself, why I wanted to keep the meeting between Elrod and me from my counselor. I think I felt as if I was protecting him from something he shouldn't know as my attorney. If it turned out that way, Sid couldn't be held responsible.

18

A PIECE OF THE PUZZLE

Elrod's patrol car was parked in my driveway when I arrived. He got out and met me at my truck by the time I stepped onto the ground.

"What's happening, Mr. Jones?" I was smiling, but Elrod apparently was not in a mood for pleasantries.

"It's gettin' a little bit complicated for me, Delbert."

"What do you mean?"

"I can't be on both sides. I'm s'posed to be investigatin' a murder that you may be involved in, and I'm s'posed to be goin' to work for you. Somethin's got to give. I ain't used to playin' games with the sheriff, no matter how much I hate his goddamn guts."

I saw his dilemma but couldn't understand how things had suddenly become so unbearable for my friend. "When did you decide this?"

"When I happened on some shit involvin' the sheriff and Cecil Campbell and the sheriff's son, Josh, more than likely."

"No shit?"

"Yeah. You know that new house of Loudermilk's out on the point? Well, I heard some pretty sound talk that a bunch of materials in that house came from your company."

"How'd you find that out?"

"Talkin' with Jared Barlow."

"At Southern Building Supplies?"

"Yeah, tells me that several times his drivers delivered materials to your worksites and were instructed to leave the trailer. Later, when they delivered to the Loudermilk site, they saw your trailer with those same materials parked there."

"This is a damn good time for him to say something. Where in the hell has he been for the last year while I been paying his company twenty thousand dollars every month?"

"Like everybody else, Delbert, scared shitless of Sheriff Loudermilk. That's why he didn't say anything."

"I'm not the bravest son of a bitch in the world, but I don't think I've ever been too scared to allow my customers to be scammed."

"Ain't Barlow's fault really, Delbert. Not everybody swings the hammer you got."

"It's not the hammer, Elrod. It's the balls."

"Anyway, he told me now. And he knows he's riskin' his ass."

"I would have turned it up sooner or late I already have an outside accountant doing a forensic analysis of financials. I started that as soon as I learned Cecil had disappeared."

"There's somethin' else. Josh Loudermilk was supplyin' Campbell with drugs. At least that's what I've heard."

"Wonder what the sheriff knows about his son's activities."

"I don't know, Delbert, but I mean to find out."

"What do you want me to do?"

"Is that job at the ranch still open?'

"Whenever you're ready."

"How about today?"

"You're hired," I said. "Go back and tell fat ass you quit."

Now, Elrod was smiling. "When can I move into the house?"

"Not for a while. There's evidence in that house the sheriff hasn't even bothered to check. I'll tell you about it after you're no longer an officer of the law. And don't worry about Josh Loudermilk; leave him to Colonel Holt and me."

We shook hands and Elrod hurried to his patrol car. I pulled my truck to the side so he wouldn't have to drive on my lawn. The damage caused by Harlan Haynes was just starting to heal.

I ASKED JOSIE TO WHIP UP A SNACK FOR ME, THEN called Marge Wilson and let her know I couldn't make it to dinner. "I may have something really good for your campaign."

"What's it about?"

"Can't say right now, but it may drive a nail in the sheriff's coffin."

"I can't wait to hear it.""You'll have to, lady, but if I'm right, it will be worth the wait. By the way, I still want some more of your meatloaf."

"Any time, Delbert. Just let me know. Be sure to catch our new ad that starts this evening on all three channels. It has some great details in it that should really get responses from the sheriff."

"What's the ad about?'

"We're just highlighting a slew of improper and unfounded arrests made by the sheriff or Harlan Haynes that were never prosecuted for lack of evidence. And we point out at least three suits pending against the sheriff right now for false arrest. That doesn't include your lawsuit. We are asking the question: why won't our courts put those cases on the docket?"

"And what's your answer to that question?"

"Because the sheriff has most of the local judges and county prosecutor in his pocket."

"Damn, lady. I guess you do mean to shake up things."

"There needs to be some housecleaning in Cumbersome County, especially in Maysville, and I'm the person to do it. You told me so yourself, Delbert. Oh, I forgot to mention we will be making street-by-street loudspeaker tours all next week and a meet and greet each Saturday right up to the election."

"Good, Marge. Sounds like you have it going in the right direction, and that's good because I'm up to my eyebrows trying to solve a couple of murders."

"I saw the report about the burned-out truck on Highway 57. I understand the Mississippi Bureau of Investigation is involved in that, so maybe you won't have Loudermilk breathing down your neck on that one."

"The bastard still won't let go. Wants to make himself a hero."

"Have you or the colonel made any progress on that?"

"Not much, but enough to know that our friend, Gerald

Hinson, is right in the middle of it. You heard anything about him since he was in jail a couple of weeks ago?"

"Nothing, you know, Ballard paid his bail, and as far as I know. Hinson just disappeared after that. At least he hasn't been arrested again."

"I'm looking for him too, along with my former foreman, Cecil Campbell. So let me know if their names crop up at the sheriff's department."

As soon as I finished my dinner, Luis and I inspected the electric gate installation. From the looks of things, I expected the fence and gate to be completed by the end of the week. Afterward, I got into my truck and headed for the ranch. It was nearing feeding time, and I was hoping to hook up with Vicky Metzger. I owed her for overseeing the ranch for a few days. We had not discussed a price, but it was my intention to make it worth her while. I also wanted to let her know that Elrod would be running things at the ranch for me starting the following morning.

A sheriff's patrol car was pulled into the circle, but no one was in the car. Stu McCarty came running from the barn. He passed me without speaking. I called his name and ran after him. Taking him by the arm, I turned him to face me. "Where in the hell are you going in such a hurry, Stu?"

"That damn woman threatened to shoot me."

"What woman?"

"That Metzger woman, Logan's old girlfriend."

"What in the hell are you talking about?"

"She's in the barn now, threatened to shoot me with that pink .380 she carries."

I had to laugh, thinking *you're one hell of a lawman.* "Jesus, you've got a bigger gun than that in your holster."

"Wouldn't look very good, would it, if I shot someone in your barn? We already got one unsolved murder that happened out here. I sure as hell wouldn't want to get drug into that."

"What'd you do to piss her off?"

He turned back toward his patrol car and began walking with me right behind him. "She didn't threaten to shoot your ass for no reason. What the hell is going on, Stu?"

"Nothin'." He continued to his car, got in, and peeled out of the driveway.

I walked on out to the barn. The tack room door hinges creaked as it opened. Vicky looked startled when she turned to face me. She was holding a handkerchief to her mouth. She pulled it away and held it to her side. I could see bloodstains on the handkerchief and a small abrasion on her lower lip. She turned away quickly and busied herself with the bridles and paraphernalia on the wall.

I spoke to the back of her head. "What's going on, Vicky?"

"Nothing that concerns you."

"What happened between you and Deputy McCarty?"

She turned to face me. "I don't want to get into it."

"Doesn't have anything to do with Logan Vice, does it?"

"Where did you get such an idea?"

"Just a lucky guess."

"How much did you guess?"

"That you lied to me."

"Why do you say that?"

"Well, for one, you told me Logan Vice was a pretty boy, not your type."

"He wasn't my type, but I found that out too late."

"It kinda puts a different face on things, don't you think?"

"I don't know what you mean."

"It must have put you at odds with Carmen. She was bedding down your pretty boy, wasn't she?"

"Don't try to involve me in that." She picked up her hat and walked into the barnyard. I followed.

"You involved yourself in this mess, lady. And I want to know what was happening between you and Stu McCarty?"

"Do you think I would have anything to do with that little pocked-face bastard?"

"Frankly, Vicky, I don't know what to believe about you. Why is Stu McCarty slapping you around?"

"Who in the hell do you think you are, Mr. Cantrell? I don't have to answer your questions."

"Maybe you'd prefer to answer questions from the state police. They're getting involved, you know. Maybe the FBI also."

"I don't have anything to hide from them, but I am not going to discuss my personal relationships with you."

"Have it your way. But tell you what—I'm paying you to help out here at the ranch, five hundred dollars for the week if you think that's fair. And I'm giving you two weeks to get your horses off my property."

She put her hands to her face, and I thought she would cry, but a moment later, she regained her composure and looked at me, exasperation evident in her voice. "I don't want to move my horses. But I'm not going to let you embroil me in your personal affairs. I was aware that Logan Vice had something going with your wife at one time. But that was over when we began seeing each other. So, I had no reason to be jealous of Carmen Cantrell."

"All right, then tell me what was happening between you and McCarty."

She crossed her arms and was silent for a moment. "How well do you know Logan Vice?"

"I know he's a goddamn creep."

"And I know that better than you."

"When did you decide that?"

"If you want to know the truth, I have known all along, but had it confirmed for certain today."

"Did Deputy McCarty have any part in that?"

"Yes, he was the messenger; came to tell me Logan didn't think we should see each other again."

"Damn coward," I said. "Didn't have the guts to face you."

"The real insult came in the way McCarty delivered the message. He offered to console me after breaking the news from Logan."

"What happened?

"He tried to kiss me. When I resisted, he bit my lower lip. I pulled my derringer from my back pocket, grabbed my bag, and showed it to him. That's when he ran like hell for his patrol car.'"

"Yeah, he was in a hurry when I met him on the way in."

"I think I would have shot the bastard if he stayed here. I shouldn't let him get away with it, but I don't know where to turn."

"You need to make a police report."

"To Sheriff Loudermilk? A lot of good that would do."

"No, but you have an attorney, don't you?"

She nodded.

"Let him handle it for you."

"I can't do that. The whole thing is complicated. I think Logan told Stu McCarty I was his for the taking."

She went back to the tack room and I followed. I was having second thoughts about her taking her horses off the ranch.

She began filling two pails with feed from sacks tagged with her name. We didn't speak for two or three minutes. I kept thinking about how strong she was. Most women would have cried a little even if it was just for effect, but not her. She was either too tough or too stubborn to let her emotions show.

"I'm sorry, Vicky. Forget what I said about your horses—I was just pissed at the moment."

She didn't answer but continued to mix feed for her horses. I wondered if she knew how enticing her derriere was as she bent over the feed buckets.

She looked up to see me watching her. "Like what you see?"

"Yes, I sure as hell do. But I know what kind of trouble it could lead to."

"Me too, but who gives a damn?"

"I do, honey. There's one thing I don't need right now, and that is more trouble."

"I am a difficult woman, but I can be as sweet as pie when I want, and I'm offering." She came close and stood, her breasts touching my chest.

"And I'm not refusing." I pulled her close and kissed her, tasting the blood from her lip. She was warmer in my arms than I anticipated. I let her go and stepped back. "That's enough. I'm sorry I did that. I don't need more troubles right now."

"Why did you start something you don't know how to finish?"

"I know how to finish it, honey, but not now. Maybe we can talk about it later."

"Maybe." She picked up the two pails of feed and walked from the tack room toward the stalls in the back of the barn. I'll bet she knew my eyes were still fixed on her ass.

I drove home wondering what piece of the puzzle I had just stumbled onto. I kept thinking that I finally reeled in Vicky Metzger and had her right where I wanted. Or was it the other way around? Maybe I was the one being reeled in. *Nah, I'm too smart for that.*

19

THE TRUTH WILL SET YOU FREE

I made the rounds on Tuesday morning, meeting first with Eddie Mayfield to go over three upcoming bid packages and working out the details for starting a small construction project in Satsuma, Alabama. Then I drove to Leakesville to check the progress on the strip mall being constructed there. The trip took me across Highway 57, past the dirt road where we found my burned-out truck. For a moment, I thought about driving up the road to see the site again but changed my mind. I drove on past but kept thinking about the man who died inside my truck. Who was he? Was he still alive when the vehicle was set afire? Those questions brought me to thoughts of Shirley Campbell. I couldn't shake the idea that she was a whole lot more involved in the man's murder than she admitted. *Something doesn't ring true about her story. Maybe she hasn't lied, but she sure as hell hasn't told me everything.*

In Leakesville, Dooley seemed to have the job well under control. He told me he needed some supervisory help and wanted to promote a good worker by the name of Al Benton. I understood that Dooley was shorthanded since he was handling both his and Campbell's jobs without an assistant. Once that was settled, I let Dooley know that he and Eddie Mayfield would be on their own for at least a week, maybe more. I was planning to catch up with Colonel Holt and start making better progress solving Carmen's murder. I was sure I would fill him in on my Vicky Metzger encounter. But first, I needed to drop in on Shirley Campbell.

The three dogs came yelping from under the house and surrounded my truck before my feet hit the ground. I growled at them, and they scattered, heading for their shelter. They continued to bark, with only their muzzles protruding from under the house.

I walked up the steps and surveyed the porch for ashtrays and cigarette butts or other indications that Cecil had been on the premises since my last visit, but there was no evidence of that. I rang the bell and waited. A few seconds later, the curtain on the window nearest the front door moved. I was sure Shirley had peeked out to check on her visitor, but I heard no movement from inside the house. I knocked on the door and waited a minute longer. "Shirley. Delbert Cantrell. I need to talk with you."

The dogs set up a chorus, their barking louder than ever. If she didn't hear me calling, she sure as hell heard the dogs. I banged on the door. "Mrs. Campbell, I need to talk with you."

The door opened a few inches, and Shirley spoke to me through the small opening. Only her nose and mouth were visible to me. "I'm not dressed. Can you come back?"

"No," I said. I'll wait."

"Suit yourself." She closed the door, and I took a seat in the porch swing. The dogs stopped barking and came onto the porch. I called to them, and they came to the swing, all three of them plopping down close to my feet.

Five or ten minutes passed before Shirley opened the door and came onto the porch. She sat in a rocker a few feet from me, still disheveled. It was apparent the events of the past few weeks were taking a toll. "Mr. Cantrell, I don't mean to be disagreeable, but I'm growing mighty tired of everybody asking me questions."

"Who, besides me, have you talked to?"

"Well, for one, Deputy Elrod Jones. That was a few days ago. And, yesterday, two officers from the state came."

"Were they state troopers?"

"They showed me their badges but weren't in uniform."

"What did they ask you?"

"If I knew where my husband was, and they asked if I had any information about the corpse that was burned in your truck."

"What did you tell them?"

"Nothing. I told them the same thing I told Deputy Jones."

"What was that?"

"That the last time I saw Cecil was over a week ago."

"But you've seen him since then."

"I don't know what you're talking about."

"You know, Shirley, I've been giving this a whole lot of thought. I just can't see Cecil having anything to do with Gerald Hinson, GG, as you called him. I think you lied to me about that."

"I didn't lie."

"Look, I'm still willing to protect you and your boys, but only if I know the truth. Had you ever met Gerald Hinson before that day?"

"No, but the way you described him, I'm sure it was Hinson."

"But you never heard Cecil call him anything other than GG?"

"No, but don't you think it was him?"

"I don't know, but intend to find out if you will just tell me everything."

"And what do you think that is, Mr. Cantrell?"

"I think Cecil came home alone on Tuesday morning before daylight. He told you he killed someone, maybe Gerald Hinson, and set my truck on fire. He was driving the man's truck, which he needed to dispose of. You followed him to wherever he dumped the truck, then drove him out of town. Cecil hoped everyone would think he burned in my company truck."

She put her open hands to her forehead and sobbed.

I gave her a few minutes to regain her composure, then I asked, "Am I right, Shirley?"

"Almost."

"Tell me about it."

"I don't want to go to jail. What would my boys do?"

"I'll help you every way I can. But I don't think you have much choice. Now, tell me the truth."

"It was close to midnight when Cecil drove up in your company truck. He told me he had killed a man over a drug deal and had to dispose of his body. He got a can of gas from the shed. I followed him to a dirt road out on 57, where the police later found the truck."

"Where was the man's body at that time?"

"Still in the back of his truck. Cecil removed the brush he had put there, then drug the body off the back of the truck."

I shook my head in disbelief. "And hauled it down the road about two miles before setting my truck on fire?"

"Yes," she said. "Then he put the man's body inside your company truck."

Her efforts to continue talking were disrupted by almost continuous sobbing.

"It's all right," I said. "Take your time, but tell me what happened next."

"I don't know. I couldn't watch. The next thing I knew, flames were coming from the front seat of your truck."

"And the man's truck is in the marsh?"

"Yes, it's covered with brush."

"Where did you go then?"

"I drove him to the bus station in Slidell."

"Where was he headed?'

"San Antonio, then Mexico." She continued sobbing, breaking up her words.

I had an urge to hold her, console her, slap her, and break her goddamn neck all at the same time. But I got up from the swing and walked to the edge of the porch, searching through my mixed emotions. "Damn, that must be hard for you to live with."

"It's awful, Mr. Cantrell. And I feel dirty, like I deserve to be punished, but I don't know what will become of my boys."

"What you did can't be excused, but I don't think you had much choice."

"I could have refused to help him. But I could only think of the boys and what might happen to them if Cecil went to jail."

"Did you think he was going to get away with it?"

"I couldn't think beyond that moment."

I stood, looking out over the yard toward the road that wound its way around several live oak trees down to the main road, thinking of what I would have to do next. The Campbell house sat on a raised knoll amidst a beautiful grove of pecans and oaks, belying the scheme by Cecil Campbell to commit murder. You hear of such things on the news, but when it is someone you thought you knew so well, it makes you lose faith in human beings. I took a handkerchief from my pocket and wiped my eyes, which were clouding with the makings of tears. *You're not so tough after all, Mr. Cantrell.*

We were at least a week from any possible DNA results on the burned corpse. I became aware that Shirley had gotten up from the rocker and was standing near the edge of the porch beside me. Tears were still wetting her eyes. I placed my arm about her shoulder. "It'll be all right. Stop worrying."

Her voice was sincere and apologetic. "You're a good man, Mr. Cantrell, and I'm so sorry Cecil did you wrong."

"Don't worry about me. Employees are like husbands or wives; they can break your heart when you have too much faith in them. It isn't the first time it's happened to me—all part of doing business. But for you, it is outright betrayal.

The man used you and left you to deal with the mess he created."

I thanked her and walked down the steps.

She called after me. "Where are you going now?"

"San Antonio."

20

A FULL PLATE

On the way home, I called Colonel Holt. He was just sitting down for an early dinner with his wife.

"Delbert, I was planning to call you right after supper. Got some lowdown on Hinson. I thought we should get together tomorrow."

"Can't be tomorrow. I'm getting ready for a trip,

"Where to?"

"Mexico."

"Mexico? You got a lead on our man Campbell?"

"I don't know for sure, but I'm going to find out."

"Are you leaving early tomorrow?"

"Yes, and I've got some things to go over with you. Can you drive out to my house when you finish dinner?"

"I was planning an evening with my family. Can't we do it first thing tomorrow morning?"

"Not unless you want to meet at 4 a.m. I'm heading to New Orleans at five to catch a flight to San Antonio."

"Do you want me to go with you?"

"It would be good to have company, but I think one of us needs to stay here. We'll talk about it when you get to my house."

"Seven OK?"

"Yeah, great. See you at seven."

My thoughts went back to Shirley Campbell. I believed she had been as honest with me as her heart would allow. Still, I felt almost certain she held something back, something that would lead me directly to her husband. That notion was one of the things I wanted to discuss with Colonel Holt. We needed to learn if she was communicating with Cecil by phone or other means. In spite of the dire circumstances Cecil had caused his family, I thought she would continue to help him as much as possible. That was a situation we needed to monitor and one that I would place in the colonel's hands while I was in Mexico looking for Campbell.

Colonel Holt arrived promptly at seven. I invited him into the den, where Josie served coffee and a slice of her homemade apple pie.

"Nice place, Delbert. Looks like you're making a fortress with that wrought iron fence you have going up."

"Yeah, a $39,000 investment just to keep out the goddamn sheriff's deputy."

"Which one?"

"That half-brained Harlan Haynes. Came beating down my door in the middle of the night. Parked on my lawn and dug up ten feet of it when he peeled out of here. That ain't going to happen again. What really gripes my ass is that I was dumb enough to follow him into town and allow him to slap a pair of handcuffs on me."

I could see that Isadore was amused, but he allowed a mouthful of apple pie to suppress any urge he might have had to laugh.

While we finished our coffee, I told the colonel about my visit with Shirley Campbell and the concerns I had that she had not been completely forthcoming. "I wonder if you can find out about her phone calls. See if she is communicating with Cecil."

"Delbert, I'm going to let you in on something I wouldn't tell anyone else. Colonel Stanley, the Director of the Mississippi Highway Patrol, is a good friend of mine. We both attended Tuskegee. He doesn't run the crime lab but can get a man to work with me to find out who was burned in your truck. He'll be working with the feds." He laughed. "You may run into them in Mexico. Just make sure they don't mistake you for Mr. Campbell."

"Yeah, I know, Colonel, you're going to say all us whites look alike. But they won't ever mistake me for Campbell if I find him before they do because he's going to have two broken legs."

"I expect Colonel Stanley will keep me informed of what the feds are doing. Maybe we should put off the Mexico trip until we get something from them. What do you think?"

"Well, to be honest, I think you're trying to tell me I'm screwing up by going there now."

"I didn't exactly say that, but it would help to have some solid info before we go."

"The problem is that you work from facts, but I run on

instinct. And something tells me I'll be able to find that son of a bitch. I can do it before the FBI can, and I'm not going to wait on them."

"I doubt you can find him before the FBI does. You don't have their resources."

"And they don't have my friends."

"Who's that?"

"I have a friend in Mexico City. He has amigos all over that country, and they all owe him favors."

"How is he going to be involved?"

"He'll meet me wherever I end up in Mexico, and he'll get the word out to all his men. We'll need photographs and descriptions. I'll get my VP, Eddie Mayfield, to send that to me by email before I get to San Antonio."

"Are you going to Mexico City?"

"I don't know, probably not. I suspect Campbell will go someplace into the interior and get lost for a while."

"I hope you don't spend a lot of money on a wild goose chase."

"Maybe I will, but you'll be doing some chasing of your own while I'm gone."

"By the way, I ended up against a brick wall with that woman, Vicky Metzger."

"So did I." I didn't elaborate. "She's a real puzzle to figure out. But Shirley Campbell is another story. She's still got something she wants to tell us. But we can't let the feds know how much she may be involved in this whole damn mess."

"You know, if they intercept her calls, they may find out themselves."

"If they do, they do, but I promised her I would keep her out of it if possible."

He grinned. "Delbert, you got something going with this gal?"

"'Course not. It's just that she's been shit on every way from Sunday. And she's got two young boys that need a parent."

"I'll do my best," he said.

"There's one more thing, and it's a dilly"

He leaned forward to catch my every word.

"This one involves our illustrious sheriff and Cecil Campbell."

"That ought to be good."

"Yeah, guess I was helping him pay to build that Taj Mahal out on the point."

He looked puzzled.

"You know where it is, Colonel, out there off 98 east of Maysville."

"Oh yes, I've noticed that going up for almost a year."

"Well, as it turns out, Mr. Campbell was buying materials charged to my projects but delivered to Sheriff Loudermilk's worksite."

"How do you know this?"

"Elrod Jones."

"Damn."

"Here's what I want you to do. Get the complete story from Elrod, then pay a visit to Jared Barlow at Southern Construction Supply. He knew what was going on but didn't do anything about it."

"Did he explain why not?"

"I haven't talked with him, but Elrod did. I guess Barlow

was scared shitless of the sheriff. But I want you to get all the facts together. We'll take them to Saperstein and watch the fireworks from there."

"All right, Delbert. Looks like you're filling my plate before you go."

"I'm not finished, but first, bring me up to date on Hinson."

"That's really what I wanted to talk to you about."

"What have you found out?"

"Bro, this dude's a real piece of work. Been married three times, has four or five kids he doesn't take care of, and has been arrested a dozen times, three for DUI, a bunch for dealing, and once for armed robbery. That was dismissed. There was something about arson, but I didn't get the full story on that. Apparently, he is still married to the lucky third Mrs. Hinson, but she says she hasn't seen him in more than six months."

"I think he's skipped bail on his last DUI and driving on a suspended license. Ballard Bonding is on his tail, I'm sure."

"Only one good thing, Delbert."

"Yeah?"

"His DNA and prints are on file. I found that out. If it was Hinson in the truck, we'll know in a couple of weeks. Meantime, we keep looking."

"That's something else I wanted to talk about. According to Shirley Campbell, there is a four-wheeler trail a couple of miles further up that dirt road from where my truck burned. She says there is a swampy area back in the pines and that an old truck is at the end of that trail, covered with brush. If it has a license plate, it should lead us directly to the owner. If not, we should be able to trace the VIN. The owner of that truck was probably the burned corpse."

"Well, Delbert, you're making sure I stay busy while you're gone, aren't you?"

"What the hell else you got to do, Colonel? Have dinner with your wife and kids?"

He shrugged. "Once in a while couldn't hurt."

I got away from that subject as soon as possible and began talking about Elrod Jones. "Keep your night guard on until I get back from Mexico. Elrod will be there during the day."

I excused myself for a moment, went into my office, and returned with a ring of keys. "Something to add to the plate. These are the house keys for the ranch. I want you to go out there one evening and search Carmen's office for a will, bank ledgers, checkbooks, or other documents."

"She probably kept the will in a safe deposit box, wouldn't you think?"

"I don't know, but if she did, there's a key to the box someplace."

"What are you worried about?"

"Not about the ranch. It was owned by both of us, and I paid cash for it. But if she died intestate, there's probate and a hell of a mess Saperstein will have to handle."

"Speaking of Saperstein, what did he advise you about going to Mexico?"

"He didn't because I haven't told him."

"Are you going to tell him?"

"No. You can tell him after I'm on a plane for San Antonio."

"I get all the easy jobs, don't I?"

"Well, Isadore, here is a really easy one, and I think you'll enjoy it."

"Put it on me."

"No, nothing bad. I want to make sure Marge Wilson is getting exposure in the Black neighborhoods. Would you call the mayor of Moss Point and set up some public appearances with him?"

"I'm way ahead of you, Delbert. I talked with Marge earlier today, and I'm meeting with the mayor tomorrow. He used to work for me, you know."

"Sure, I knew. That's why I asked you to call him." I lied through my teeth but couldn't let the colonel get ahead of me on every issue.

IT WAS GETTING DARK WHEN ISADORE LEFT MY driveway. As soon as his car was out of sight, I made a call to my friend, Carlos Aragon, in Mexico City. I asked him to be ready to meet me at one of our border crossings on a day's notice. Carlos held dual citizenship in the US and Mexico. He was fluent in English and Spanish and made frequent transits between the two countries. I met him more than ten years earlier when he was peddling construction equipment in the US.

He suggested I drive to Laredo since it was almost due south of San Antonio. "You can rent a car in San Antonio and drive straight down I-35 to the border. If I were trying to get lost in Mexico, I would find a place to cross between Laredo and Brownsville."

"Ok, my friend, I will be in San Antonio about 11 a.m.

I'll call you then. Why don't you plan to come to Nuevo Laredo, and we'll start the chase from there."

"Who are you looking for? You got pictures?"

"Yeah, I'll be sending those by phone when I get to San Antonio. I'll give you the complete lowdown when we meet in Nuevo Laredo. Let your boys know we'll spread a little green for their troubles, including ten thousand to the guy who brings in Campbell alive."

"What do you have against this guy? What's he done?

"Fucked my wife, stole from me, probably killed a man, and burned my fucking truck."

I attempted to keep talking, but Carlos was laughing so hard and muttering shit in Spanish that I couldn't get a word in. When he took a breath in between guffaws, I said, "I'm damn glad you're taking my problems so seriously."

"No," he said. I was just wondering which of those things pissed you off most."

"When he burned my truck, that put me over the edge. I can't blame him for fucking Carmen—she was a beautiful woman and available. Stealing and murder? Who doesn't do that?"

He went into another laughing spell at my expense. When he finally got his voice back, he said, "I'm glad to see you still have a sense of humor."

"And I can see that you don't."

He turned serious. "I'll be glad to help you find this son of a bitch."

"All right, Carlos. I'll call you when I get to San Antonio."

"And I'll make sure I'm in Nuevo Laredo by day after tomorrow, midafternoon. I'll have everything ready for you,"

"Like what?"

"Plenty of tequila and cerveza. The first thing we are going to do, my friend, is throw ourselves a damn good drunk. I can see you need it, and I know I will before this deal is over."

21

———

CLOSING IN

A few minutes after Isadore's taillights disappeared, the phone rang. I didn't expect to hear Vicky Metzger's voice, but there it was. "Hi, Delbert. I was just wondering if you're busy and if you might like some company this evening."

My immediate thought was *this woman doesn't beat around the bush.* And I would have to admit I liked that about her, but there were two reasons why I was going to decline her second offer. For one, I wasn't sure what game she might be playing, and second, 4 a.m. would come way too early for a late romp in the hay. "I'm sure you would be damn good company, but I have to leave here at five in the morning."

"I could just drop by to keep you company for a while and leave before midnight."

"Tell you what. Let's keep this on ice until I get back home."

"Where are you going?"

"Dallas," I said, "to see my brother."

"Something wrong?"

"Could be. He's getting married."

She chuckled. "I know what you mean."

"And I damn sure do!"

"When are you coming back?"

"Four or five days."

"Give me a call when you're heading this way."

"Sure. I'll be in touch."

I couldn't shake thoughts of her as I packed my bag, showered, and got ready for bed. I envisioned her tight little ass in a pair of white lace bikini panties. She looked damn enticing, especially with the small devil horns protruding from her forehead. After nearly two weeks, I was still trying to figure her out. It could be she was as horny as hell and didn't care who she bedded down. At almost fifty, and half again her age, I didn't consider myself the target of an attractive divorcée. Then again, I wasn't too hard on the eyes. It could have been that she liked what she saw. But maybe she was only seeing dollar signs when she looked my way. I had to remember she was still picking the bones of her former chiropractor husband, and now she might have her claws out for me. Or all of those things could be wrong. She could be trying to blind me to her possible connections to Carmen's murder.

I finally put all those thoughts behind me and slept like a baby until the alarm shocked me awake at four. I arrived at Louis Armstrong Airport about seven-thirty and landed at Houston Hobby a little after nine. While I waited to make my connection to San Antonio, I called Carlos to see where we would meet in Nuevo Laredo the next day. We agreed on the Marriott, which seemed the prudent thing to do since most of the other hotel names were unfamiliar to me. He would lock in the reservations, with me arriving late in the evening and him coming in the next afternoon.

Before picking up a rental car in San Antonio, I checked my iPad and forwarded photographs and descriptions of Cecil Campbell to Carlos. He would get them out to his contacts as soon as he received them. I thought with that advanced information in Carlos's hands, we would be prepared for our search for Campbell, but I was to learn that my friend had other plans.

I crossed the border at Nuevo Laredo and checked into the Marriott in time for a late dinner in my room. After showering, I called room service for shredded beef enchiladas and frozen margaritas. My waiter was accommodating, not only delivering my meal in less than half an hour but also suggesting where I could find the prettiest senoritas in all of Mexico. He pressed two fingers to his lips and kissed them. "Mui bueno." Then he volunteered in perfect English, "And not expensive."

I shook my head. "Not tonight, gracias."

"I can call now, and they will come right over."

I declined his offer but tipped him as if he had just lined me up with Penelope Cruz. "No thanks, not tonight." I signed my bill and handed him a fifty. I thought he might be a good man to know.

He shook my hand vigorously. "If you change your mind, my name is Jesus." He smiled and pointed to the name displayed above his pocket.

I had some calls to make right after dinner, the first to Carlos. "I'm here, already fed, and propositioned."

"Don't settle for hamburger, my friend. I have arranged for us to have filet mignon tomorrow."

"Where are you digging up that meal?"

"In Villa Juarez, and they are beauties."

I knew Carlos had an uncle living in El Paso. "Are you going to El Paso first?

"No, not Ciudad Juarez. I'm talking about Villa Juarez, a little town about sixty miles from Laredo. We will drive there and party for a day or two. If you want the girls to come back to Laredo, they will."

"Are they as nice as Penelope Cruz?"

He laughed as only Carlos can, a deep rumble from way down in his chest. "Sisters," he said. "They are Penelope's younger sisters."

"And you know these girls?"

"One of them very well. The other—I've seen pictures, and she will knock your socks off, my friend."

"I'd love that, but how about waiting a couple of days for the girls? We have a lot of work to do."

"Delbert, I haven't seen you in more than two years. We need to celebrate first with a damn good drunk. So, I'll see you tomorrow afternoon. Get your party clothes on."

"Can't wait."

I owed Elrod an explanation of what was happening, so I got him on the phone and explained why I was in Mexico. I instructed him not to let Vicky know where I was. "She thinks I'm in Dallas attending my brother's wedding."

"He getting married? I thought he was funny."

"What do you mean by that?"

"You know, Delbert, funny."

I could have jumped his ass a little but had to consider

that he was a well-meaning good ole boy. He would have trouble digesting any explanation I might offer. So, I let him know he just needed to keep things turning at the ranch. "If you need money, call Saperstein and have him advance funds to you. Give me a couple of days before you do that. By then, I will let Sydney know where I am and what I'm doing."

I waited until the next day to call Saperstein. My thinking was that while Carlos and I were being entertained by two beautiful senoritas, Sydney would be wondering if I had fallen off the face of the earth. I preferred to wait a couple of days longer to drop my surprise on him but knew he would be calling me, perhaps at a most inconvenient time.

"Cantrell, where are you?"

"Right here," I said, "talking with you on the phone."

"Yes, but where are you?"

Before I could answer, he continued. "I just told Carolyn to see if she could hunt you down. I have some information that will complicate your life even more than it is."

"What's that?"

"The crime lab called. They finished the DNA on the samples you and the colonel brought me."

As I prepared to listen, I decided I would have to disappoint Carlos and his girls. Saperstein's first statement had made me decide I would be returning home the next day instead of getting drunk. "What are the results?"

"The DNA on one cup matches DNA collected from Carmen's corpse and her panties. The other cup has DNA from an unknown female."

"I'll bet I can guess who that is."

"All right, Sherlock, who is it?"

"Vicky Metzger. Am I right?"

"Still unidentified, but she might be a good starting point."

"You can bet your ass on that, Counselor."

"Maybe, but the other news is that the blood sample belongs to an unidentified male."

There was silence on the phone. I supposed Sydney was waiting for one of my explosive reactions, but my mind went in too many directions to form a cohesive question.

Sydney continued. "Of course, we have to turn over this information to the state. And you know they'll be swarming the house and ranch once this is laid on their plate."

The vision of my burned-out truck came to mind. "Do you think the blood sample will match the DNA of the victim in my truck?"

"It's a possibility but doesn't help you, Delbert. It just brings more suspicion your way."

"I don't see how."

"If it's his blood in your wife's bedroom and his corpse in your truck, you don't come away looking like Pope John the Twenty-Third. Anyway, Delbert, you need to come in so we can talk—and bring the colonel with you."

"I can't do that right now, Sid. I'm indisposed."

"Where?"

"In Mexico."

"What are you doing in Mexico?"

"Investigating. I was going to cut my visit short but changed my mind with your news. So now, the first thing I am going to do is get drunk. While I'm drunk, I am going to fuck a Mexican beauty, and then I'm going to find Cecil

Campbell and kick his ass all the way back to Cumbersome County, Mississippi."

The phone went silent. I assumed Saperstein hung up.

Next morning, after breakfast, I called Colonel Holt and told him about my phone conversation with my attorney. "I don't think he's too happy with me right now."

"Do you want me to smooth his feathers? I probably need to check in with him anyway, get the complete lowdown on the forensic reports he got from Dr. Schmidt."

"Good. If I learn anything at all, I'll give you a call."

"Delbert, before you go, let me bring you up to date on the sheriff and Southern Construction Supplies. I've talked with Jared Barlow and can tell you for certain we've got the goods on the sheriff. Barlow will provide records and will testify."

"How did you manage that? The last I heard, he was hiding under a table, scared to death of the sheriff."

"I got him to watch Marge Wilson's commercials. He's convinced now that she will be our new sheriff, and he won't have to worry about Loudermilk."

"And he went for it?"

"More than that, he has videos of the materials being transferred from his trailer to the sheriff's. One of the men is a sheriff's deputy, maybe the other one too."

"Damn, that's good. Which one?"

"You'll never guess."

"Ten to one, it was Logan Vice or Stu McCarty."

"On the money, Delbert with Vice, but I don't know who

the other person is. The video is shadowy and doesn't show his face. But as soon as I can get a meeting with Saperstein, I'm going to let him know what evidence I've found."

"What about Hinson? You got anything more on him?"

"Nothing. The man has disappeared into thin air."

"I'll bet his latest wife knows where he is. Have you made another run on her?"

"I tried, but she professed ignorance. You may need to talk with her when you get back into town. I think she's a little suspicious of a Black man."

"I don't know when that will be—maybe four or five days."

"It will just have to wait until then with her. No use wasting my time."

"Before you go, Colonel, there's one more thing. We're looking for another missing man, no idea who he is, but I'm betting his DNA matches the corpse in my truck."

"What makes you think that?"

"The blood sample you took from the bed didn't come from anyone we know."

"Who then?"

"An unknown male. But my gut feel is that it will match the dead man."

"Does Saperstein know this?"

"Yes, Colonel. He's the one who told me about the lab report. Also, one of the coffee cups matches an unknown female. Bet your mind goes the same place as mine on this one."

"You mean Miss Metzger?"

"You bet your ass I do."

"I'm sorry to say, but I feel as if I'm about to start this investigation all over."

"Not me, Colonel. I think we're closing in on a whole nest of rattlers, and we'll start defanging the bastards as soon as I sober up."

I heard the colonel get the first syllable of my name out of his mouth before I shut off my cell phone. I needed time to get ready for my date with Penelope's younger sister.

22

PLEASURE BEFORE BUSINESS

Carlos's flight came into Laredo, and I met him at the border crossing. I had almost forgotten how much I loved my fat friend, who I had not seen in more than two years. During the past ten years, we teamed on three or four small construction projects just outside of Mexico City with him acting as my attorney, dealing with the Mexican government. He was as smart as anyone I ever met, and was once the district attorney of the state of Durango at twenty-four years old, the youngest district attorney to ever serve in Mexico. He knew which wheels needed greasing and kept them rolling while I stayed out of the picture back in the States.

Looking at my pudgy little friend, you might not consider him much of a Don Juan, but he always seemed to be in the company of a beautiful young woman, usually introduced as his attorney. He played hard, but when it was nut cutting time, he got down to business.

I waited outside my car while Carlos was processed

through Customs. A broad smile crossed his face as he approached. I extended my hand. He grasped it and pulled me toward him, rising to kiss the side of my face. "I love you like a brother, my friend."

As we embraced, I said, "Same here, Carlos. It's great to see you again."

I threw his bag and briefcase into the trunk while he sank into the front passenger seat. The twenty-minute drive to the hotel gave us a chance to catch up on the main events of our lives since we last saw each other.

"I almost got married two years ago," he said, "but she caught me with someone else a few days before our wedding date."

"And she didn't have a sense of humor, I guess."

"Not much. She told me she never wanted to see me again."

"How did you feel about that?"

"It hurt for a while. Her padres are very wealthy people, mostly her mother. Cost me four hundred thousand pesos to settle with her."

"Why was that?"

"She was suing me—claimed I stole her daughter's virginity."

"Did you?"

His laughter rumbled up through his throat. "No, she gave it to me."

I laughed, too, as he continued. "They all thought I had more money than I do. So, when they learned the truth about my finances, they were glad to get rid of me, with or without their daughter's virginity. We settled out of court, but it still cost me almost four hundred thousand pesos in legal fees and payoffs."

"What happened to the girl?"

"Marina?"

"Is that her name?"

"Yes. She went to Texas and found a husband who doesn't give a shit about virginity. She's married now, so we're all happy. I still see her once in a while when I go to El Paso, but her parents don't know."

"That sounds like a nice arrangement."

"The problem is that I'm still poor."

"But single—and happy."

"You should know about that. Aren't you happier since you're single again?"

"My situation is a little different from yours. I guess I qualify as a widower since Carmen is dead."

"I thought you were getting a divorce."

"We were, but it was held up because we couldn't work out a property agreement."

"Is that why you killed her?"

"I guess that's what a lot of people think, but at least one son of a bitch knows it's not true, and that's the reason why I'm in Mexico."

Carlos slapped my shoulder. "And we're going to find him."

I stepped on the gas, revving the engine for a moment. "Well, let's get going."

He chuckled. "Not so fast, my friend. Pleasure before business. First, we're going to get you fucked."

∽

WE ARRIVED IN VILLA JUAREZ ABOUT FIVE THAT evening, just in time to get caught in the midst of a traffic jam led by a white van blasting mariachi music over loudspeakers. We followed it through town to a square populated with live oak trees, treated with whitewash at least four feet up the trunks. We turned onto a street lined with a row of recently constructed three-story white stucco buildings. Carlos motioned for me to park alongside the curb of the narrow street.

"We'll put the car in the garage later."

"Is this your idea of a whorehouse?"

"No way, my brother. This is my attorney's home and office. You might not remember, but you met her once in Austin four years ago." He smiled. "She was doing some legal work for me."

"I do remember. We were staying at the Regency, right? Her name was Natalia, as I remember."

"Yes."

"She's a beautiful young lady."

"And her sister is just as beautiful. Her name is Isabella. You will meet her shortly. She's a schoolteacher."

We took the girls to dinner. By the time we returned, the streetlights were on, and soft ballads played over loudspeakers in the park no more than two blocks away. Back in the apartment, we mixed margaritas and turned on banda music. After a third round of drinks and a few attempts at dancing by all of us, Carlos and Natalia disappeared into her bedroom. That left Isabella and me to get better acquainted.

My Spanish was good for saying good morning, good afternoon, and where's the bathroom? Isabella's English was better than my Spanish, and with a few more rounds of margaritas, we made ourselves comfortable for the remainder of the evening. About midnight, I took her by the hand and led her to the other bedroom. She lay back on a pillow, fully clothed, looking up through her dark eyes at me.

I had never seen anyone as beautiful and alluring since my first night with Carmen. That thought and the realization of all the problems a beautiful woman can bring a lonely man made me want to run, but I couldn't resist the dark beauty lying on the bed. I wanted to know her better. I lay down beside her and reached for her hand. I turned my face to hers and kissed her lips as tenderly as I knew how.

"I'm sorry," she said.

"Why? What have you done?"

"Perhaps I've misled you because I can't make love to you, you know."

I looked at the angelic face of Isabella and thought she couldn't have been more than twenty-two or twenty-three years old. I said to her, "How old are you?"

"Twenty-five," she said. "I've never looked my age."

"Am I older than you expected?"

"No," she said. "It isn't that."

"Then why are you here?"

"For my sister."

"Did she tell you about me?"

"Yes. Said you're a nice man."

"Why don't you want me to make love to you?"

"Because I am still a virgin."

"At twenty-five?"

"Si, Senor Delbert."

For a moment, I thought about kicking down the door to

Natalia's bedroom and telling Carlos we were getting on the road back to Nuevo Laredo.

"And still a virgin?"

"Yes. You don't believe me? I swear to you."

"But why? Don't you want to ever make love to a man?"

"Yes, but only after I marry. Would you marry me, Senor Delbert?"

"That's sure as hell out of the question."

"Lo siento mucho."

"I'm sorry too, but you must have known why you were coming to meet me.".

Tears filled her dark eyes. "No, por favor, Senor Delbert. My sister said there would be no sex. If I am not a virgin, I will not get a good husband."

She was sobbing when I left the room. I sat, looking at the wall, thinking about yanking Carlos out of bed and giving him hell. After twenty minutes or so, I cooled off and returned to the bedroom with what was left of the last batch of margaritas. I sat next to the bed, holding Isabella's hand. We both drank from the glass. When the drink was gone, I got into the bed beside her and held her. After a few minutes, she was asleep. I turned out the light and continued holding her until morning.

I was awakened by music coming from down the hall. I lifted Isabella's head and freed my arm. Carlos was sitting at the counter, sipping coffee, his ass hanging over the sides of the bar chair. He was wearing a green-and-red checkered robe. He lifted his arms in the air as if to say, "Tell me about it."

"There's nothing to tell."

"Nothing to tell? You slept with one of the loveliest senoritas in all of Mexico, and you have nothing to say, not even a, 'Thank you, my friend?'"

"Carlos, sometimes you can be a hard-hearted asshole."

"Are you angry with me?"

"No, should I be? The least you could have done is to tell me she's a virgin."

"Not anymore, I would bet." He smiled and raised his eyebrows as if to ask, *no?*"

"No, she's still a virgin, and she will remain that way as long as she's with me."

"You surprise me, Delbert. But you also make me proud that you're my friend." He got off the chair and grasped my hand.

I made a mock fist and shook it at him. We both laughed. "You know, Carlos, when I was younger, nothing would have stopped me from having sex with that beautiful young woman. But she's almost half my age. I just couldn't pressure her to do something she would regret forever."

In spite of my comments about his hard heart, I knew Carlos to be warm and caring, a wonderful friend. His kindness was always evident in his large, dark eyes. He slapped my shoulder, then went to the stove and began preparing breakfast. Neither of us spoke for a while.

When the aroma of chili powder and onions filled my nostrils, I asked Carlos what he was preparing for breakfast.

"Migas, and you will love them, my friend."

I stood and peered over the bar.

"No, no," he said, "I want you to be surprised. Call the girls. We're fifteen minutes away from breakfast."

After breakfast, Carlos and Natalia returned to their bedroom, leaving Isabella and me to share an uneasy hour watching television, most of which I could not understand because of my poor Spanish.

"I am sorry to disappoint you, Mr. Delbert."

Before I could respond, she continued. "I didn't intend to spoil your reunion with Carlos, but I just couldn't go through with it."

"That's OK. I'm not upset with you."

"It isn't you," she said. "I think you're really nice. But no man will want me for a wife if I'm not a virgin. And I would have to make confession to the padre."

"It's all right. I think you're wonderful."

"If you want, I will leave today."

"Where will you go?"

"Allende, where I teach school."

"Allende?"

"San Miguel de Allende. It's beautiful there."

"I'll bet it is, but don't leave now. You can leave tomorrow when we do. Maybe we can drive you there."

"What will we do today?"

"Tell you what. I'm going to take you shopping for clothes and something special—jewelry, whatever you want."

She came across the room, stood on her toes, and kissed my cheek. "You are a very sweet man, but I couldn't let you do that."

"Yes, you can. There won't be any obligation. I know you don't make a lot of money as a schoolteacher, and I want to help."

She kissed me again on the cheek. I put my arms about her waist and held her close to me. With her head resting on my chest, we stood in the center of the room holding each other. I could have fallen for her so easily, but I refused to allow myself to have such thoughts.

We celebrated that night with dinner in town and more margaritas and dancing when we returned to the apartment. Not wishing to tempt fate, I slept on the couch that night and awoke Saturday morning with a crick in my neck. I think I called myself a stupid son of a bitch. However, I was rather proud of myself. It was good to know I had placed someone else above me—a rare event in my life. Somehow, I knew it would be difficult to get the Mexican beauty out of my mind.

23

—————

BACK TO REALITY

We drove Isabella to Allende and went on to Nuevo Laredo, arriving midafternoon. There was a message at the hotel desk from Colonel Holt. As soon as I got to my room, I returned his call.

"What's up, Colonel"

"I hope you're getting something done in Mexico because you're holding things up here."

"How so?"

"Well, I found the truck in the pine forest swamp just as Shirley Campbell said, but it isn't an old junker—it's a new Chevy Silverado."

"When did you find it?"

"Last evening, and I suspect I'm not the only one who knows it's there. Someone has removed brush from around the truck, maybe getting ready to haul it away or strip it."

"Have you notified anyone?"

"No, I posted a guard on it while I found out who owns it."

"Any luck?"

"You know a guy by the name of John Williams from Hattiesburg?"

I couldn't help but think *how in the hell did he get in the middle of this?* "Yeah, sure do. He's a pointy-toed cowboy. He was Carmen's live-in boyfriend when I met her. She shit-canned him for me and my money. I can assure you he has no love for me at all."

"Well, Delbert, my man, I don't think he loves anyone any longer. It's his truck, and I'm betting it's his blood on Carmen's mattress and his corpse in your truck."

"Damn, I didn't even know he was back in the picture."

"Talking about pictures, you want to know what I think happened the night Carmen was killed?"

"I have my own theory, but let me hear yours, Colonel."

"I think the killer probably heard that Williams was back with Carmen and made a surprise visit to the ranch. He found Williams sleeping in her bed. Carmen came home just as the murder was taking place. We can guess the rest."

"Close, I guess. But where does the female DNA come in?"

"I haven't figured that out yet, but she could have had coffee with Carmen earlier that evening."

"You still think it's Metzger's DNA?"

"Who else?"

"I don't know, but we need to talk to her again. When I get home, I'll invite her over to see my etchings."

The colonel laughed. "Is that what they call it?"

"That and other things."

"What makes you think she'll come?"

"I'm guessing she hates to be turned down."

"Maybe, but I don't know what you're implying."

"Well, Colonel, she's offered twice, and I declined both times. The last offer is still pending."

"Seriously, Delbert, you need to get back here as soon as you can."

"I'm wrapping up here over the weekend and will be back in Maysville Monday evening."

"I'm calling Colonel Stanley at the highway patrol to get his team down here going over the truck before it disappears. Should I also call Saperstein?"

"Yeah, guess so. He'll be pissed if we don't. But I know what he'll say, that the Williams connection only makes things look worse for me. Sometimes, I think he believes I'm guilty of something. Anyway, he'll want to notify his friend, Dr. Schmidt."

"He's just playing devil's advocate like any good lawyer, unless of course you really did have something to do with it." He had a good chuckle, making me realize how well we had bonded in less than two weeks.

"OK, Colonel. Try holding things together until I get back there on Monday. I expect the feds and state investigators will be swarming the truck as soon as you notify them. I hope they've got Sheriff Loudermilk and his department under investigation. You might want to check with Colonel Stanley on that situation."

"I don't know how much he'll be willing to tell me about Loudermilk. They keep those investigations of law enforcement close to the vest."

"At least you have enough to keep you busy. By the way,

email me an invoice, and I will cut a check for you when I get home Monday. I imagine I owe you a good chunk by now."

"Yeah, enough to pay the rent. Oh, Delbert, I almost forgot to mention my call to Shirley Campbell yesterday. She wouldn't come right out and say it, but I'm confident she has spoken with her husband recently. I don't think she quite trusts me. Maybe you should give her a call."

"I'll do that and let you know what I find out. If she's heard from him, and he's in Mexico, I'd like to know that. Anything else?"

"No, except you'd be proud of Marge Wilson. She held a news conference yesterday and lambasted the sheriff for under-the-table dealings. I'm convinced she'll win in November if he doesn't put a hit on her."

"That's not out of the question, you know."

"He should know he couldn't get away with it."

"I'm not so sure. He has gotten away with everything else so far."

"But the noose is tightening, my man. I can assure you."

"I hope so. You and I both know he's a slippery bastard."

THE NEXT THING I DID WAS CALL SHIRLEY CAMPBELL. I began the conversation by telling her to go to the company office on Monday. "You know Eddie Mayfield, don't you?"

"Yes, I met him at one of the company picnics—him and his wife."

"Eddie will have a check ready for you to help you through the next couple of weeks. Stop by right after lunch. I imagine you can use the money."

"Yes, we sure can. Thank you, Mr. Cantrell."

I let her think about my generosity for a moment before getting down to the reason for my call. With John Williams in the mix, it seemed unlikely to me Shirley took part in Carmen's murder, but it didn't eliminate her culpability in helping Cecil dispose of the body. And it only complicated my theories of Gerald Hinson's involvement. What about the female DNA and the lady with the classic little ass advertised in her bootcut cowgirl jeans? How did Vicky Metzger, Cecil Campbell, and Gerald Hinson fit together? It might be that demure Shirley Campbell held the key, and I aimed to find out.

"Shirley, I need your help."

She was quiet. I hoped she was stewing in the implications of that simple statement. I allowed her a moment or two longer for contemplation before saying more.

"Shirley, did you understand me?"

"Yes," she said. "I understand."

"Do you understand what I'm asking you to do?"

I waited for her response until my impatience took over. "You know he's going to get caught."

She didn't comment.

"You know he's going to get caught, and you're going to be right in the middle. You'll probably go to jail."

She said nothing for several seconds, but gave a deep sigh of apparent resignation. I think she realized there was no choice but to tell me everything she was hiding.

"You need to think about what will happen to your boys if you and Cecil both end up in prison."

"I've thought of that." Her words were almost whispered.

"Let me ask you, have you ever heard the name John Williams?"

"Oh my God, you know!"

"Yes, I know, and so do you. It was his body in the truck."

She attempted to speak, but her voice broke. After a few seconds, she tried again. "He ... ruined our lives."

"Who? John Williams?" I knew she meant Cecil, but I wanted to hear her admit it.

"My husband."

"I know. And don't you think it's time you stop protecting him?"

"Yes." She appeared to be overcome by intermittent sobbing.

"Will you tell me the truth about what happened?"

"Give me a little time."

As I waited patiently for several minutes, her sobs gradually grew inaudible. "You need to tell me, Shirley. I'll help you all I can."

She cleared her voice and began. "I don't know everything but understand that Cecil went to the ranch late on that Thursday evening. John Williams was an old boyfriend of Carmen's. He had forced his way into the house. He and Cecil got into a fight, and Williams drew a gun. According to Cecil, they wrestled over the gun, and the man was shot."

"I don't think it happened that way but go ahead and tell me Cecil's version."

"Cecil said he called his buddy, Gerald Hinson, to help dispose of the body. They put Williams in his truck, and Gerald drove it to Highway 57 with Cecil following. They drove Williams's truck into a bog with the body in the back and covered it with brush and branches.

Did he mention Carmen or a woman by the name of Vicky Metzger?"

"Not Vicky Metzger, but Cecil did mention Carmen. He said she promised not to tell anyone."

"Then why do you think someone killed Carmen?"

"I don't know, but Cecil said she was OK when he and Hinson left that evening."

"Does that story make sense to you, Shirley?"

"I don't know. Nothing makes sense anymore."

"When did you next see your husband?"

"I didn't see him until Sunday, I think, after news of Carmen's murder. He came home and said I had to help him disappear, that he would be blamed with both murders."

"Why didn't he get his buddy Hinson to help?"

"I think he said Hinson had been arrested for something else. And, anyway, he didn't trust him enough to let him know about his plan to disappear."

"Has he called you recently?"

"Yes, three times. He called from San Antonio once."

"When was the last time you heard from him?"

"Yesterday morning."

"Where was he calling from?"

"He said Mexico. Is there a Brownsville in Mexico?"

"Is that where he said he was calling from?"

"No, he just said Mexico, but I think he mentioned Brownsville."

She had given me much more than I thought she might. The information had to get into the hands of Carlos and his men and Colonel Holt. I was grateful to Shirley and told her so.

"Thanks for your help. I don't believe everything Cecil told you, but some of it makes sense. If he calls again, you have my number. Let me know. And for God's sake, don't tell him you've spoken with me."

"No, I won't."

"Go by the office and pick up your check. Eddie will have it ready for you. And call me right away if you hear from your husband."

I CALLED COLONEL HOLT AND CONFIRMED THAT JOHN Williams was the man burned in my truck. It was imperative to get that information into the hands of the state police and the FBI. I imagined the feds already had enough on Cecil Campbell to be checking all border crossings into Mexico.

Afterward, I knocked on Carlos's door. "Hola, mi amigo. Como esta?"

"Get that shit-eating grin off your face, Delbert, and tell me what's happening."

"You have any contacts near Brownsville?"

'Why?'

"Because our boy may be there, trying to get across."

"Yeah, I have a man in Reynosa and a couple in Nuevo Leon."

"Do they know who they're looking for?"

"They have all the photos you sent me. And they all want to collect your ten thousand dollars."

"How much are you paying them now?"

"A thousand pesos a day; enough to keep their interest."

"One of them may be getting close to collecting. I talked with Cecil's wife. She thinks he's in Mexico. It sounds as if he may have crossed somewhere around Brownsville, or he may still be in Brownsville for all I know."

"You have any more information I can pass on to my people?"

"I was thinking, you know, he's hooked on something."

"What?"

"I don't know, but would guess cocaine or heroin. Hell, it might be crystal meth."

"Then he'll be looking for a source."

"Exactly."

"If he's in Mexico, he came to the right place, and the price is right. All those drugs are plentiful and cheap and on every street in Mexico."

I went back to my room for a rest while Carlos phoned a dozen or more contacts from Laredo to Brownsville on both sides of the border. Just for insurance, he planned to call all his contacts from Nuevo Laredo to Cuidad Juarez and El Paso. We couldn't risk leaving the border unguarded anywhere along the Rio Grande.

I hoped for a call from Shirley Campbell, giving me information that would help close the loop on her husband, but the call never came. About 9:00 p.m., I knocked on Carlos's door. "Let's drive to Reynosa. I think we might find the son of a bitch near Brownsville."

"No, my friend, let's wait here. I'm telling you I have every town along the border covered, and any gringo looking for drugs will be swept up in our net. It may take time, but if he's in Mexico, we'll find him. You and I need to get some sleep before all hell breaks loose. It could happen today; it could happen tomorrow, but we'll find him."

I returned to my room, lay back on a pillow, and with visions of Isabella running through my mind, fell asleep with my boots on.

24

DON'T BELIEVE EVERYTHING YOU'RE TOLD

The serenity of Saturday morning ended right after breakfast when I checked my voice messages and found a day-old scolding from my lawyer. "Delbert, this is Sydney. You must be in Timbuktu; either that or you are just ignoring my calls. I want to talk with you but don't want to have the subject matter on your voicemail. I'm on my way to Temple now and will be in meditation the rest of the day until midnight. Call me Sunday evening after six—that's 6 p.m., Delbert, not a.m. I don't want you calling early and pissing off both me and my wife."

I always relished a good ass-chewing from Sydney. It made me realize he still had my interest at heart.

While I was wondering what was in his craw, my phone rang. It was Shirley Campbell. "Mr. Cantrell, I got a call from Cecil early this morning. He's broke and wants me to send money to him in Rio Bravo."

"Is he in Mexico?"

"Yes. He said Rio Bravo, Mexico. I think it's close to Brownsville. He left there yesterday."

"How are you supposed to send the money?"

"By Western Union. He wants two hundred dollars, but I'm not going to send it."

"I think you should send something, maybe fifty dollars, but give me about four hours to find Rio Bravo on the map and drive there. We'll be there when he picks up the money at Western Union."

"He wants me to send it to someone else by the name of Emilio Sanchez. How will you know who that is?"

"I don't know, but we will. Just get on the phone and wire the money in about three hours. You can use your VISA card."

"All right," she said, "I'll be sending it about two, my time."

I brushed my teeth, combed my hair for a second time, and then walked three doors down to Carlos's room. He opened the door with his right hand while his left reached to get his arm into the sleeve that was dangling from his shoulder. "Damn," he said, "I thought you were room service."

"Jesus bringing you something?"

"Who is Jesus?"

"Bellboy, waiter, pimp—depends on what you want. Don't tell me he hasn't tried to fix you up yet."

"Nothing from Jesus. I ordered a pitcher of margaritas. Want a liquid lunch?"

"No, thanks. I had enough in Villa Juarez to do me for a while. Call down and tell the kitchen to put your drink in a thermos. We're going for a ride."

"Where to?"

"Rio Bravo. Know where that is?"

"Does a bear shit in the woods? But what's in Rio Bravo?"

"We're going to collect a Western Union wire transfer. Finish getting dressed, and I'll tell you all about it on the way there."

On the one hundred-eighty-mile drive I explained my call from Shirley Campbell. "Do you think we can find out about the transfer? You know Western Union is pretty tough on security. We may just have to stake out the locations and wait for our man to pick up his money."

"Yeah," Carlos said "But first, we go to one of the stations and make sure money is coming in to Emilio Sanchez in Rio Bravo. That sounds fishy to me."

"You won't be able to find that out. We'll have to have someone wait at each pickup station."

"That may be the case, but I want to know if the money is coming into Rio Bravo. You know it can be picked up anywhere as long as there is proper identification."

"I don't know how you'll find that out."

"My friend, this is Mexico. For fifty dollars, I can have anyone I want killed. So, I know I can get the information we need."

Carlos got on his iPad and searched for Western Union pickup locations. There were four listed. We went to the first one on the list. I waited in the car while Carlos worked his magic. After fifteen minutes, he returned. "There's no money coming to Emilio Sanchez in Rio Bravo or anywhere else. The girl checked for Cecil Campbell just in case, but nothing for him either. Maybe you'd better call Mrs. Campbell and find out what happened."

Five minutes later, I had Shirley Campbell on the phone. "Did you send the money?"

"No," she said, "They wouldn't take my VISA."

"I've driven almost two hundred miles for nothing. Why didn't you call me?"

"I tried, but your phone kept going to voicemail."

"I didn't get any messages from you."

"I don't know why you didn't. Maybe I called a wrong number."

My short fuse was beginning to burn, but I resisted the urge to explode on hapless Shirley Campbell. "Never mind. We'll send Emilio fifty dollars from Rio Bravo and see if Cecil surfaces. We'll need a phone number for him so Western Union can make notification."

"I don't have a phone number for Emilio Sanchez."

"How about Cecil? Do you have a phone number for him?"

"No," she said. "He's using throwaway phones. The last number I had was 281 855 8585, but it doesn't answer any longer."

I think I might have choked her if she had been close enough. "Didn't you know you can't send money without a contact number?"

"No. I haven't sent money by Western Union in years."

That sounded curious, considering her urgent call to me that morning. I wanted to believe she had not intended to mislead me, but there was a nagging suspicion on my mind that Shirley just wanted to know where I was. And I fell for it. I checked my voicemail. There were no messages except an old one from Saperstein asking that I return his call. It had been made on Friday, but not erased. I made a mental note to check my voice messages more frequently.

I started the car and pulled away from the curb. "I think we've been had."

"Your first time by a woman?"

I shook my head and stepped on the gas.

"Not my first time either, but you've got to wonder what kind of game your Mrs. Campbell is playing." He opened the thermos and filled the cap. "Too bad you're driving, my friend."

I drove like a bat out of hell back to Nuevo Laredo, arriving a little after five. My plane was scheduled to leave from San Antonio at 11 a.m. the next morning. That meant an early alarm and off to the races. While Carlos sipped his diluted margarita, I thought of my hero, Pete Pitchfork, and wondered how he might handle my situation. Pete would probably shoot his way out, but hell, I wasn't even carrying a gun.

WE ATE DINNER IN THE HOTEL RESTAURANT, A NICE T-bone and salad. After a glass of Grand Marnier, I went back to my room and called Saperstein.

"What's up, Counselor?"

"You must be afraid I'm going to charge double for long-distance consultations. Why have you been so hard to reach?"

"I told you I was going to get lost for a couple of days so I could get drunk and get laid."

"How did that go?"

"Well, I did manage to get drunk."

"Delbert, my man, it's time to get sober, and what I'm about to tell you may just do the trick."

"Believe it or not, but I've already been shocked back to sobriety by my friend and beneficiary, Shirley Campbell."

"Wonders of wonders! What did she do?"

"Lied to me."

"The news I have for you should make up for that. I don't know how much I should tell you because I don't want to breach attorney/client confidentiality, but I think you know a deputy by the name of Stu McCarty."

"I sure as hell do. He's a dipshit."

"Maybe, but he may also be my client. I haven't decided if I will have a conflict representing him. If I take him on, I'll be representing two dipshits."

"You're getting to be a regular comedian, Sid. Tell me, what has old Stu done now?"

"He needs a lawyer—wants to turn state's evidence."

"About what?"

"His Boss. Like I said, I don't know how much I should tell you right now. But word got out that there's a criminal investigation involving Sheriff Loudermilk and Southern Construction Supply."

"How'd that get out?"

"Word gets around. I guess Jared Barlow must have done some talking out of church."

"And Stu wants to sing to save his ass?"

"That's right, Delbert, and he may be singing more than one tune."

"You could have a whole chorus of deputies before it's

over, almost in harmony. I'll bet they will be jumping ship like the rats they are. It couldn't happen to a nicer guy than John Loudermilk, and just in time to make Marge Wilson a shoo-in."

"Don't forget about Harlan Haynes. I hear he's polling ahead of the sheriff."

"I'm not concerned about that little weasel. I suspect he'll also be a member of the deputy chorus." I laughed and even pulled a small chuckle out of Sydney Saperstein.

"When will you be home? We need to get together with the colonel and make all the pieces fit. I will decide tomorrow if I can take on Stu McCarty as a client. No matter what he's done, he can't be nearly as interesting a client as you and not nearly as much of a headache."

"Go ahead and take him on, Sydney. Hell, who knows, Stu and I may become bosom buddies, and we'll owe it all to you."

"Do you have anything else to say that's worth my time, Delbert?"

"Your time, Counselor? And all the while I thought you were billing me for this conversation."

"I am. Goodbye, Delbert."

"Goodbye, Sydney. I'll call you when I land in New Orleans tomorrow afternoon." I took comfort in believing he admired me as much as I admired him.

CARLOS AND I WENT TO THE BAR FOR A FEW DRINKS before our reunion came to an end. Our table was close to the dance floor in the middle of the room, where two flamenco dancers performed to music played by a four-piece mariachi band. The horn player was louder than he was good, but all in all, the music was not bad, considering there was no cover charge. Jesus was still propositioning but at a reduced price. Perhaps he realized it was Sunday evening and his last chance to make a commission from a gringo with money to spare. When he brought us our next drink, I compensated him for his persistence by dropping an extra twenty onto the serving tray. A few minutes later, I noticed him in conversation with another customer in the corner of the cantina, and I silently wished him success. He didn't try to make a sale with me for the remainder of the evening.

On the way to our rooms on the fourth floor, I said goodbye to Carlos and thanked him for all his help. "I've already taken care of everything at the front desk, and there's an open account for you to make any charges you desire. When you figure up your expenses, give me a call at my office, and I will transfer the money to your account."

"You don't owe me anything, my friend."

"Yes, I do, more than you might realize. One day, I will explain it to you."

"It doesn't involve a beautiful senorita, does it?"

"One day, Carlos, I'll tell you. But I insist on knowing what your expenses are for the past four or five days."

When we got off the elevator, we embraced and said our goodbyes. "There's no reason to wait two years until we see each other again. You have to come to Mississippi and spend a week with me."

He opened the door and, just before disappearing behind it, promised he would see me soon. *Soon* came much quicker than I expected, in fact, it was at 4 a.m., just an hour before my scheduled wake-up call. My room phone rang. It was Carlos. "They've got your man."

"Who has my man and where?"

"My contact on the US side in El Paso spotted him and notified your Border Patrol. Customs has him in detention now."

"Damn, I need to get there, but have to fly home tomorrow. Can you go to El Paso and make certain it's our man and that the officials have the complete lowdown on the son of a bitch?"

"I'll be there by early afternoon. I'll call my uncle and have him meet me at the airport. He has good friends in the Border Patrol and Customs. Guess what alias he was using?"

"Not Emilio Sanchez."

"You got it, my friend."

"Looks like Shirley Campbell loves her man a whole lot more than he deserves. She made sure we were 900 miles from El Paso while Cecil was trying to get across into Juarez. She probably thought we would spend a week there looking for him. That pathetic little woman is a whole lot more cunning than I imagined. It's too bad for her that she couldn't think of another Spanish name besides Emilio. That mistake may land her a few years behind bars. It really tied her in with Cecil's plan to disappear."

I could envision Carlos shaking his head at my gullibility. "It's too bad that you are a sucker for women, Delbert. You can't believe everything they tell you."

I knew it was true but wondered about all the implications in his statement.

25

THE HOUSE GUEST

The drive up I-35 to San Antonio gave me the peace and quiet I needed to put things in perspective. One thing for certain, I was through playing games with Shirley Campbell. She was in the mess with Cecil all the way up to her ears. And she had played me for a fool. I would confront her soon, but not before I solved other parts of the puzzle. The first step in that direction would depend on the results of Carlos's trip to El Paso. I expected to know something about that as soon as my plane landed at the Houston airport. The next step would entail a meeting with the colonel and Saperstein first thing Tuesday morning. But there was another person I wanted to hear from for more than one reason—Vicky Metzger.

After an hour or so on the freeway, I called her. She answered so sternly I almost jumped out of my boots. "Metzger here."

"Vicky, I'm on my way home from Dallas. I called to

invite you for dinner at about eight tonight. I hope I haven't called too early."

"Delbert?" I could tell she was pleased and probably surprised to hear from me.

"Yes."

"When will you be home?"

"Not later than six if my planes are on time. I'll call if I'm going to be late."

She played coy. "How long do you expect dinner to last?"

"As long as you like. You are welcome to spend the night in the guest suite."

"Will I be safe there?"

"Probably not."

"Good," she said.

"You know how to get to my house?"

"Who doesn't?"

"Eight then."

"Yes, see you at eight."

I called my housekeeper and asked her to prepare a nice dinner for my overnight guest. Josie said she would have to go to the market but would fix something special. "Is it a lady friend?"

"Does it matter?"

"No, but if it's a lady, I might put flowers in the guestroom."

"All right then, it's a woman. I'll find out later if she's a lady."

Josie laughed. She was a couple of years younger than me but treated me like her son sometimes.

I asked. "Did the fence get finished?"

"Yes, Friday, and I hate it."

"Why?"

"Because I keep forgetting my remote and can't remember the code."

"That's ridiculous, Josie. You have to get used to it. It'll keep you safe."

It was obvious she had heard enough when she abruptly ended our conversation. "I have to go now. There are a lot of things to do before your guest gets here this evening."

I arrived at the San Antonio airport just before ten and checked in for my flight before calling Saperstein's office to confirm our meeting on Tuesday. His secretary told me Sid had an early court appearance, but he had set our meeting for 11 a.m. the next day. "He has an appointment at nine, but that should be over before eleven."

Intuition told me he was meeting with Stu McCarty. "Who's he meeting with?"

"You know I can't tell you that, Mr. Cantrell."

"It isn't Stu McCarty, is it?"

"I can't tell you, but do admire your instincts, Delbert."

"Thanks, Carolyn, now I owe you lunch and dinner."

Before I got on the plane, I contacted Colonel Holt and briefed him on the turn of events with Shirley Campbell and her husband. I wanted to mention McCarty but thought it best to allow the colonel to be surprised if that subject was brought up by Saperstein the next day.

"An all-points bulletin has been put out on Cecil Campbell," he said. "So, I wouldn't be surprised if the FBI is not already on the scene in El Paso. Yesterday, the Mississippi state investigators retrieved Mr. Williams's truck and hauled it away for evidence. I think that takes one mess off our hands."

"All right, Colonel, I have to get down to my gate. I'll see you tomorrow at Saperstein's office at eleven."

The flight took all of forty-five minutes, leaving me with more than an hour before my plane departed for New Orleans. I attempted to contact Carlos, but his plane was in the air. I walked down to my gate and waited for the boarding call. Viewing CNN on the overhead TV monitor was like watching grass grow. They were still projecting the flight path of the lost Malaysian Airlines plane and speculating about the spot in which it landed in the Indian Ocean—damn interesting stuff. I closed my eyes, attempting to take a nap, but thoughts of Isabella kept running through my mind. I punched her into my phone, but I decided not to complete the call. What I wanted to say to her was much too personal to be heard by the other passengers waiting near me. After an hour of rotting, I boarded my flight. Maybe Vicky Metzger would help me get Isabella off my mind.

THE TIME WAS APPROACHING THREE O'CLOCK WHEN I claimed my bag. I found my Lincoln Continental on the third floor of the parking garage and weaved my way through traffic onto Interstate 10. I called Vicky and confirmed that dinner was on at eight, but she was welcome to arrive early since I expected to be home by 6 p.m. Next, I called Carlos to see what he had learned in El Paso. His report only deepened my suspicions of Shirley Campbell's role in covering for her husband.

"My uncle was able to learn that Border Patrol is holding a man with a phony passport claiming to be Emilio Sanchez. His biggest problem is that he doesn't speak one word of Spanish. I expect that we will know something more by tomorrow morning."

"Are you staying in El Paso?"

"Yes, at least for a couple of nights. I'll be at my Uncle Rene's. Of course, you can get me on my cell anytime."

I arrived home a little before six, showered, and got ready for my guest. At seven-thirty, she called from the gate. I pressed the button, allowing her to enter the property. When she pulled into the circle, I turned on the front lights and went down the steps to meet her at her car.

She handed me her small overnight bag as she pressed the remote to lock her car. She was wearing jeans and a white western shirt with bold red and green floral arrangements. I led her down the hallway toward the guest suite at the other end of the house. "Nice," she said, "very nice, and where do you sleep?"

"Upstairs."

"What if I want to talk to you?"

I pointed toward a white speaker on the wall. "There's an intercom. Just push the button for the master bedroom."

"Will you come running?" She chuckled.

"Only if you're in danger."

She noticed the flowers Josie had placed on the dressing table and bent to smell them. Smiling, she looked up at me. "You don't miss much, do you, Delbert?"

"The flowers were my housekeeper's idea. She thinks of everything." I didn't want Vicky to think that I was trying too hard to impress her.

"Let her know I appreciate the flowers." I detected disappointment in her voice.

"You can tell her at dinnertime. It will be ready soon. Do you need to freshen up?"

"Yes, it will only take a few minutes."

"I'll wait for you in the den."

She stood on her toes and kissed me firmly on the lips. I pulled her toward me and returned her kiss. For a moment, a small demon inside my head took hold. I thought of pulling the jeans down off her shapely little ass, screwing her until her eyes bulged, then telling her to get the hell out. But my suspicions of her motives held my emotions in check. There were questions I hoped Vicky Metzger would answer before the night was over. By the time the kiss ended, my little demon had taken flight. I said in a voice as sultry as I knew how, "See you at dinner."

Josie served baby lamb chops with roasted potatoes, asparagus, and carrots. The presentation was worthy of the Gulf Coast's finest restaurants. Both Vicky and I heaped praise on the talents of my housekeeper.

After dinner, we had coffee and a dessert of key lime pie in the den while we watched reruns of a British comedy on public TV. About ten o'clock, Vicky excused herself and said, loud enough for Josie to hear in the kitchen, "I'm going to bed if you don't mind. I've had a long day." She laughed quietly. "It started with you waking me before seven this morning if you remember."

"Oh, I remember," I said, "It just shows you how eager I was to take you up on your last offer. Does that still stand?"

"I wouldn't be here if it didn't."

Shortly afterward, Josie called from the kitchen. "I'm leaving now, Mr. Delbert. What time do you want breakfast?"

"Early, say seven, Josie. I have a busy day ahead of me tomorrow."

By then, Vicky had disappeared down the hall. I went up to my room and changed into sleeping shorts, all the while, wondering where our little cat and mouse game was headed, and I wasn't even sure which one of us was the cat.

Half an hour later, Vicky called on the intercom. "All right if I come up?"

"No, I'll come down."

I didn't hurry, wondering what might be going on in her devious little mind. I had been intimately acquainted with many young, beautiful women, each of them unique and complicated, but I had never met one quite like Vicky Metzger. She appeared cool, aloof, and overly independent when we first met, and she still exhibited those characteristics except in the moments she had shown her vulnerability by offering herself to me. I could see that I was doing the same by accepting her offer. I told myself I was doing it to learn how much she knew about Carmen's murder, but I couldn't deny that I was eager to see if I could tame the shrew. I knocked on the guestroom door and went in without waiting for her to respond.

She was wearing a short lavender chemise with matching panties, both trimmed in white lace. She raised her arms, her palms upright and turned all the way around. "Like what you see?"

I motioned for her to come to me. "I would be a fool if I didn't." The problem with that statement was that for the moment, I meant it. And I knew I couldn't allow that to happen, not if I wanted to win the game.

She took me by my hand and led me to her bed. "You can do anything to me you want. Anything."

It was after midnight when we lay back on our pillows. We were quiet for a few minutes before she spoke. "Where do we go from here?"

That brought me back to reality. I raised my head and rested on my elbow. "What do you mean?" I knew without asking, but I wanted her to suggest a meaningful relationship between us. She did, and that was when I knew I had prevailed in our skirmish.

"I think you and I would make a great team," she said. "I'm beautiful, intelligent, and determined. You're bright, ambitious, and easygoing, don't you think?"

"And I'm rich, and you don't know me very well. I can be a real son of a bitch when I need to."

"I don't give a damn about your money, and I can be a bitch, but not tonight. Let's make love again." She kissed me.

I stroked her hair. "Let's just talk for a few minutes."

"About what."

"The situation at the ranch. How well did you know Carmen?"

"Well enough. She was a really nice person and a good friend but an awful businesswoman."

"We can agree on that, but what do you think happened to her?"

"Believe me, if I knew, I would have already told someone. Carmen and I talked often."

"What about?"

"Horses, mainly. And men. It was getting crazy—the last few weeks, a different man there almost every evening. I was honestly concerned for her."

"Why were you scared?"

"She was too trusting—all those guys coming and going. There were bound to be fights. And there were. You know Logan Vice."

I nodded. "Uh-huh."

"He was a real troublemaker. He thought he was God's gift to women. I think Carmen told him to leave and not come back. But I'm not sure he got the message."

"When we first met, you said you barely knew him, but I heard you had a fling with Mr. Vice."

"I wouldn't call it a fling, and I wasn't proud of it. It didn't take long to discover he was a real asshole."

"Did you know any of the others?"

"Not well," she said, "but I was acquainted with a few."

"Did you know Cecil Campbell?"

"Yeah, I knew him. He would come out to the barn with Carmen. Seemed like a real nice guy. I knew he was married. You know, that was something about Carmen—she liked married men. I think she liked knowing she could steal a man from another woman. That's one of the things that concerned me."

"There were others?"

"Yes, a real jerk by the name of Gerald Hinson. He was there often, sometimes with Cecil. Oh yes, and there was the sheriff's young son, Josh. He had a huge crush on Carmen."

"She didn't have anything going with Josh, did she?"

"No, I'm sure she didn't, but he liked hanging around her, and I think she enjoyed the attention. She helped him with his horses—showed him how to groom and saddle them. She might have given him some riding lessons, too, but not while I was at the ranch."

I sat up in bed so I could look more directly into her eyes. "Tell me, when was the last time you saw her?"

I could see the question evoked memories difficult for her to think about. "The evening before they found her body. We sat on the back steps and drank coffee. She said an old friend was coming over, and he may spend the night. She didn't tell me his name, and I didn't ask. Girls have a way of understanding there are things they don't need to know."

"How late did you stay?"

"I left just before dusk. After coffee, I checked on my horses and then left the ranch. I would say that was a little after seven. You don't think I had anything to do with her murder, do you?"

"No, but you might have seen something that holds the key to finding her killer."

"Like what?"

"I don't know, something odd that happened that evening."

"If I can think of anything, I'll let you know, Delbert.'

"Just one more thing. I know it was getting dark, but was Carmen wearing sunglasses?"

As she answered, a sad smile crossed her face as if it hurt her to think about it. "I wouldn't say she was wearing them. But you knew Carmen. She always had those sunglasses perched on the top of her head, winter, summer, daylight, or dark. They were a part of her outfit." She paused, smiled, and started talking again. "The sunglasses were like her coffee cup—she always had the glasses in her hair and a cup of coffee in her hand. She was laid back and beautiful and remarkable in her own way. I will miss her."

I pulled her close to me and kissed her forehead. We made love again, and I removed Vicky Metzger from my suspects list.

26

WHERE'S CECIL CAMPBELL?

After breakfast, Vicky left for the ranch to feed her horses and let them out to pasture. I drove to the office to check with Eddie Mayfield about our Leakesville project and to make certain he would have a check ready for Shirley Campbell when she called. I wanted to avoid any suspicions on her part until the scenario in El Paso played out. I assumed when that happened, all bets would be off, and Shirley Campbell would find herself in the crosshairs of the state and federal authorities. I was sure she would have a sad, interesting story after her attempts to distract us in Brownsville while Cecil managed to sneak across the border into Juarez. I was pissed but determined to keep my cool until I had the facts that I needed to nail her pathetic ass.

Next, I drove to the ranch to visit with Elrod Jones to see how his first week as foreman was going. I also wanted to know if he was hearing any buzz from the sheriff's office, particularly about Stu McCarty or Logan Vice.

When I arrived, a state trooper's car and an unmarked black sedan were parked near Carmen's Jaguar. I assumed they had started their own investigation.

Vicky was still at the ranch with her truck pulled close to the barn. She came out of the tack room, saw me, got into her truck, and drove off without speaking. She smiled and waved as she went by. It made me think our relationship would be just what I needed—for the most part, cool and casual, but occasionally as hot as a man could stand. She was not the type of woman to fall in love with, and I sure as hell wasn't looking for that from her.

Elrod was obviously upset. "They came in here yesterday, Delbert, about two, and stayed until dark. They jimmied the lock on the back door. Christ, they hauled away all kinds of shit. I wasn't allowed inside but got a look at what was goin' on. They just got back here half an hour ago, and I guess their rippin' things apart again this mornin'."

"You have any idea what they've taken so far?"

"No, and they didn't tell me what they're lookin' for."

"I know, Elrod. It's OK. Did they show you a search warrant?"

"Yeah, they had that—showed it to me yesterday and showed it to the Holt guard when he came on last night."

"The colonel still has a man out here?"

"Yeah, just at night. He comes on at eight for a twelve-hour shift, probably don't make any more money than I did as a deputy."

Good ole Elrod was always worried about someone's welfare and never seemed to think of himself as needing, or perhaps deserving, that same kind of consideration. It was good having him on my team.

I walked to the back steps and waited. Three men, one in a trooper's uniform, carried items to the kitchen, where they placed them in black plastic bags. After a few minutes, I caught the trooper's eye. He came to the door, and we talked.

"Who are you?" he asked, giving me an impression that he had little patience for an onlooker.

"Delbert Cantrell. I own the place."

"You want to see our search warrant?"

"No, but if I can help, let me know." I could see the notice of a crime scene posted on the door, probably one out front too, but I didn't look.

"I don't think so, but thank you."

"Just to let you know, the reason you are here is because my investigator and I found DNA samples and sent them to the state lab."

"No, the reason we are here is to solve a murder."

I laid two business cards on the edge of the porch. "I think you're a little late in the game, but my number is here if you decide you want to talk to me."

I left for my meeting with Sid Saperstein and Colonel Holt.

By ten-thirty, I was getting a little edgy, waiting to hear from Carlos. I called from the parking area in front of Saperstein's office. "What's happening, amigo?"

"Nothing I can tell you. You know I'm an hour behind you out here."

"Damn, that makes it nine-thirty; thought for sure we'd know something by now."

"Sorry, Delbert, but maybe early afternoon. Uncle Rene has a luncheon meeting with his Customs friend in two hours."

"All right. I was hoping to have some information for my lawyer this morning."

"When are you meeting him?"

"I'm here at his office now."

I looked up to see Stu McCarty passing in front of my truck. He had just left Sid's office building. "Listen, Carlos, I got to go. Something important just came up."

I got out and ran to Stu's truck just as he was closing the door. When he saw me, he started the engine and powered the window down as if to say, "what the hell do you want?"

"Stu, buddy, what're you doing here?"

"Can't talk about it, Delbert."

"Well, you know, Stu, whatever it is, I may be able to help you. You been to see one of the attorneys in this building, maybe Mr. Saperstein? You know he's a very good friend of mine."

"I've been told not to talk to anyone right now. But I want to apologize to you if I've ever done anything to harm you."

"Same here, Stu. Like I said, I might be able to help you sometime, but that works both ways, doesn't it?" I preferred to reach through the window and squeeze his goddamn neck until he told me everything he knew, especially about his fat ass boss, John Loudermilk.

"I've got to go now. I will tell you somethin', though. I'm resignin' from the sheriff's department pretty soon—maybe tomorrow."

"Why?"

"I can't say, but you'll probably hear about it on the news."

I stood from the truck as he backed out of his parking space, turned, and headed toward the center of town. A few minutes later, Colonel Holt pulled up.

As we made our way to the elevator, I said, "Just had an interesting conversation with Deputy Stu McCarty. Says he's resigning from the sheriff's department."

"Did he say why?"

"He's lawyered up—wouldn't talk about it."

"I can guess, though. I'll bet it has something to do with the sheriff's theft ring."

"Whatever it is, we don't know anything about it. We'll let Saperstein spring it on us if he thinks he should."

Carolyn took us straight to Saperstein's office. We gathered around a small conference table. Saperstein began by stating the purpose of the meeting.

"Gents, I thought it would be a good idea to get together this morning to assess where we are, see what we've accomplished, and decide what we do next. As you know, this association of the three of us came about because Delbert was accused of murdering his wife...."

"My estranged wife," I broke in.

Saperstein raised his eyebrows as he continued. "Mr. Cantrell was accused of murdering his estranged wife. Our purpose was to uncover facts that would exonerate the aforesaid, Mr. Cantrell." Smiling, he nodded toward me. "And I think we have accomplished what we set out to do. We have provided the state with information and evidence that should lead authorities to the real murderer unless, of course, Mr. Cantrell is guilty as hell."

I could see he enjoyed his final comment too much, and I had to get back at him. "What do you think that would do to your stalwart reputation, Counselor, if I did kill her?"

"And mine," Colonel Holt added with a chuckle.

Obviously undistracted, Sid resumed in typical lawyerly fashion. "As we all know, our investigations have led us in several directions and prompted our involvement in issues we never expected, one of those being the death of a gentleman by the name of John Williams. Another is the apparent theft ring involving Sheriff John Loudermilk and possibly his deputies."

I added. "Don't forget the election campaign of Marge Wilson. I think none of us expected to be involved in that when we began our inquiries."

"I certainly didn't," the colonel said. "I really expected to be running my own campaign."

Sid continued. "I have very good reason to believe Marge Wilson is a shoo-in. Now, back to our issues. Are there any new developments we have not passed on to authorities?"

"I didn't tell you, but the MBI is going through my ranch property right now. They're carrying off shit by the carload, probably emptying the freezer and pantry. I told one of the troopers I think they're a little late."

"Yes, I know they're out there, Delbert, and they want to question you. I told them you would probably agree, but not without me being present."

"I don't mind. Maybe I can put them on the right track. I knew John Williams, but not very well. He was Carmen's boyfriend when I met her." I scoffed, "I should have let him keep her."

"Might have saved you a buck or two."

"Sure as hell would have reduced your income for the past two years, Counselor."

He smiled. "Back to the MBI. They know Loudermilk has botched this thing from the start, and they have no recourse but to do a complete investigation, even at this late date."

It was obvious to me that he wanted the colonel and me to back away from our investigation, leaving it in the hands of the state and FBI. "We still may be able to help," I said.

"How? What more can you do?"

"Before the day is over, we may be able to tell them where to find Cecil Campbell if they don't already know."

"What makes you think that?"

"Customs is holding a man in El Paso going by the name of Emilio Sanchez. According to Shirley Campbell, that is the alias her husband is using. I have a man there who is in touch with Customs. And we should have a positive ID before the end of the day."

"I think we should inform the MBI and FBI so they can get someone out there," Sydney said. "It may not be him, but there's no use taking a chance."

"I agree," I said. "Colonel Holt is tight with Colonel Stanley of the state patrol. He can call as soon as our meeting ends."

"Good," Sydney said. "Is there anything else we need to discuss?"

I was hoping Sydney might bring up the subject of Stu McCarty. Since he didn't, I decided to broach the subject. "I saw Stu McCarty on my way into your office this morning." I added a little lie to force Saperstein into offering an explanation. "Stu says you've taken him on as a client and that he's resigning from the sheriff's department."

"Delbert, you are a damn piece of work. You know I couldn't talk to you about a client of mine even if I wanted to."

"So, you're confirming he is a client."

"Yes, but that's because I've decided I won't have a conflict. I'm dropping your lawsuit against the sheriff and Harlan Haynes."

"Why are you doing that? I wanted to hang both their asses."

"Believe me, Delbert, what Stu McCarty has to offer will more than compensate for a piddly-ass wrongful arrest lawsuit." Sydney could have blown me away with his vast vocabulary, but he elected to placate me with piddly-ass. With that, I needed no other explanation for his dropping the suit against the sheriff.

My phone rang. I left the table and walked to the far side of the office. "Hola, Carlos. What've you got?"

"My uncle got a call from his friend at Customs. They've identified Emilio Sanchez. It isn't Cecil Campbell."

"Damn. Looks as if Cecil might have made it into the interior. Do you know the real name of the guy they're holding?"

"Yes, my uncle says his name is Gerald Hinson, and he wants to talk to Mississippi authorities."

"I'm sure he wants to cut a deal. OK, Carlos. Find out whatever else you can. I need to get busy here. Let your uncle know how much I appreciate his help. I'll touch base with you later today, brother."

Saperstein turned in his chair to look at me. "What's going on?"

I walked back to the table and sat down, my mind trying to comprehend what I had just heard from Carlos. "Colonel, you need to make that call to Jackson as soon as you can. Customs is holding Gerald Hinson, and he wants to talk to Mississippi authorities. That blows the hell out of my theories about Cecil Campbell."

I then explained everything we had learned from my connections in Mexico and El Paso.

"Maybe you're not too far off, Delbert," Saperstein said. "Hinson might have been working with Shirley to distract you while Cecil slipped across the border somewhere far away from El Paso."

"Like Brownsville, you mean?" I shook my head, not wanting to believe I let Shirley Campbell fake me away from the place he likely crossed into Mexico.

Sydney didn't appear surprised. "Is there anything new here, really? Didn't we always suspect that Cecil and Gerald Hinson were in this thing together, especially the burning of Mr. Williams's corpse in your truck?"

"Yes, there is something new. We know now that Shirley Campbell is knee-deep in this thing. I want her to tell me how she knew Hinson's alias and why she misled me. I also want to know where in the hell Cecil Campbell is."

27

BACKING AWAY

The colonel and I left Saperstein's office in his Holt company car. We drove toward the Campbell residence.

"Delbert, you know what I've been wondering?"

"No. What?"

"Where does Saperstein go to Temple around this Godforsaken county? No matter what, come Saturday, he goes to Temple."

"He's a devout man. You might not know it if you watch him in action in the courtroom, but he's really soft as a damn pussycat. And he's devout."

"Yeah, but where does he go around here to practice his religion."

"He goes to Temple in Mobile. They have a sizable Jewish community there. But why do you bring that up at a time like this?"

"I've just been wondering—been meaning to ask him as a matter of fact."

"But why now, Colonel? Don't you have enough to think about already?"

"You know what I've learned over the years? When you've got something on your mind and don't know exactly what steps to take next, you should just back away from it for a little while, maybe a minute or two at least, and think of something else."

"Is that what you call this—backing away?"

"Yes, backing away from Cecil Campbell for a minute or two. Not you, though. You're aimed like a laser. And when you have something on your mind, you won't let it go until you get it or it gets you. The problem with that is you sometimes overshoot your target."

"Damn good thing I have you, Colonel. You can do it for both of us. You go ahead and back away for a few minutes. I backed away in Mexico, and where did it get me? Now, I'm not going to stop until I find that goddamn worm."

The colonel laughed and stepped on the gas. "OK, Delbert, my two minutes are up."

The colonel looked at his watch. "A little past twelve. You want to stop at Burger King and get a Whopper?"

"Let's do it after we visit Mrs. Campbell. I don't think I could eat right now."

"Yeah, OK. Maybe we'll have time for a real meal after we finish with her. I'll buy."

"Sure," I said.

I took out my cell phone and dialed Eddie Mayfield. "Have you heard from Shirley Campbell this morning?"

"She's come and gone. Showed up here promptly at eleven, looking as good as I've ever seen her like she didn't have a care in the world."

"Did she say where she was headed? I'm on my way to her house now."

"No, she didn't say, but I noticed something odd."

"What was that?"

"Well, I walked onto the porch just as her car was leaving, and I could swear a police officer was driving her car. First thing that occurred to me was that it was Logan Vice, but that didn't make sense. So, I just forgot about it."

"Maybe it does make sense, Eddie. Maybe it does."

"Anything you want me to do?"

"Yeah, put a stop payment on that check."

"OK, Boss, but I'll bet she went straight to the bank with it."

"You're probably right, Eddie."

"You still want me to put a stop payment on it?"

"No, you'd probably be wasting your time. But don't say anything to anyone about what you just told me."

We were approaching the turn onto the road leading up the hill to the Campbell place when my phone rang. It was Vicky Metzger. "Delbert, I need to talk with you. I'm at the ranch. Can you come by here now?"

"What's it about?"

"Something you need to know about Carmen's last day alive. I've been thinking, and I may know something that will be helpful to you."

"I'm on my way. It will take me thirty minutes to get there, so don't leave."

The colonel swung his car around and drove back to Saperstein's office, where my truck was parked. On the way, I told him about my conversations with Eddie and Vicky.

"Tell you one thing, Colonel. I sure as hell want to hear what Stu McCarty has to say when he starts singing."

"I'm more interested in what Miss Metzger has to say. I'll be in my office the rest of the afternoon. Call me when you finish with her."

I smiled. "It may be a while, Colonel."

"I can imagine," he said. "Are you still going to visit Mrs. Campbell?"

"Yes, after I talk with Miss Metzger. And don't forget you owe me lunch."

I drove up to the barn and got out. Vicky was just locking the door to the tack room. Auchtung came running like he was going to eat the tires off my truck. When he saw me, he wagged his tail.

I lowered the window. "Where's Elrod?" I asked as she walked toward my truck.

She pointed to the woods. "He's out back. A couple of fiberglass rails are down on the other side of the pond."

"Get in so we can talk."

When she did, I asked. "Ok, what've you got?"

"I've been thinking about some things that happened before Carmen was killed that maybe you should know about. I told you we had coffee the evening she was killed, but I didn't tell you everything that happened."

I listened, thinking how there is an unspoken code between women. Unlike men, women confide in each other, knowing the secrets they share are safe. They get vicarious pleasures out of being in the know on outrageous and salacious things. I think they admire women like Carmen who do as they wish, no matter who is in the way or who may get hurt.

I think Vicky attempted to put Carmen's actions in the best possible light without being judgmental. "Carmen confided in me more than I've told you. I felt as if she was telling me something she didn't want anyone else to know. And I told myself I wouldn't betray her confidence. I felt even more obligated not to discuss those things after she was killed."

"Why have you changed your mind?"

"At first, I didn't think anything she told me was connected to her murder. But now, I've decided that might not be true."

"Don't worry about surprising me when it comes to Carmen. No one knew her better than I did. I adored her rotten little ass. She enjoyed the game of seduction more than any woman I ever knew. But she would give anyone her last dime. That even goes for the women whose men she stole. I won't be shocked by whatever you tell me, and nothing you say will change my feelings for Carmen. I just want to know who killed her. I owe her that much."

"She told me more than a month ago that an old flame had come back into her life. She called him the love of her life. I think she was torn between him and Cecil Campbell."

Carmen was always torn between men, but none of them really mattered, including me. As for Cecil Campbell, I think she loved knowing she could steal him from his wife—nothing more than that. She wouldn't have kept him even if she got him. I could forgive Carmen, but not Cecil. His betrayal stuck in my throat, making me all the more eager to get my hands around his. "Did she tell you the name of her old flame?"

"His name is John Williams. And while we were

drinking coffee that evening—it was a little past five—she told me John was leaving his wife for good this time. She said he left with nothing, only the clothes on his back and his new pickup truck, which he still owed on. Later, while we were talking, her phone rang. That ended our coffee clutch, and she went inside."

"I was stalling my horses, getting ready to leave the ranch, when a new black pickup truck pulled up and parked alongside Carmen's Jaguar. I was waiting to get a look at him when she came out of the house and got into her Jaguar. They drove away in Carmen's car and returned a few minutes later. I was ready to leave but curious about this guy, so I sat in my truck, watching what was going on, sort of interested in seeing what he looked like. Their arms were flailing as if they were arguing. It appeared she was screaming at him. I couldn't hear anything they said, but a few minutes later, she got out of the car, slammed the door, and went into the house through the back door. As I drove past, he was walking slowly toward the back of the house."

"Did you get a good look at him?"

"Enough to understand why she was crazy about him."

"Carmen wasn't crazy about anyone but herself."

"No, she really liked this guy. I could see that when she was telling me about him."

"Well, if it was John Williams, he's dead."

"Why do you say that?"

"Because it was his body they found burned in my truck."

"Oh my God! How do you know that?"

"There was a positive identification. It just hasn't been made public yet."

"Now I know I should have said something earlier."

"It wouldn't have helped. He was already dead, probably before Carmen was killed."

"No, I mean, I should have come forward with this information before now. I know it isn't a very good excuse, but I didn't want to get involved. I thought it would just make things worse."

"I don't think it would have made a difference."

"Maybe not, but there's more," she said. "After I got home, I continued to worry about Carmen, so I called her. She answered, saying she couldn't talk. That wasn't like her. She could stay on the phone for hours if she had someone on the line who would listen. I waited until almost ten, then called her again. When she didn't answer, I was worried, so I drove my truck back to the ranch. On the way in, I met your company truck leaving. I recognized Cecil Campbell. But his truck was followed by the man's black Chevy. I couldn't make out the driver, but assumed it was John Williams. In the past few days, I've come to believe Gerald Hinson was driving that truck. I couldn't get that image out of my mind. That's why I called you."

"Did you go on to the ranch?"

"Yes, but the lights in the house were out, and everything was quiet. The dog barked once or twice, but other than that, there were no unusual sounds. I didn't get out of my car but sat there near the barn for several minutes. I decided everything was all right, so I drove home after that."

"Why didn't you come forward when I was arrested?"

"Honestly, I thought they might have the right man and that I was mistaken about the driver of your company truck. I thought it might have been you. I wasn't about to get involved unless I was questioned."

"I'm glad you didn't tell anyone you thought I was driving that truck. I might still be in jail."

"You don't have to worry. I don't have any doubts it was Cecil Campbell I saw that night in your truck. I've thought about that a lot, too."

She took my hand as we walked back to her truck. I kissed her cheek and then watched her drive away. I imagined she felt better after clearing her conscience, but not me. My mind was full of indecision, wondering how in the hell I was going to fit all the pieces into the jigsaw. The thought occurred to me that I should back away for a minute or two, as the colonel said.

28

RESTLESS

I backed away, expecting to hear something from El Paso that didn't come that afternoon or the next day. Waiting for others to act is a difficult pill for me to swallow. It is not my nature to sit and wonder what someone else is doing or what I should do, but rather to get off my ass and get it done. I busied myself with other matters, visiting Dooley at our construction site in Leakesville and working over a bid proposal with Eddie Mayfield for a new construction project for one of the casinos in Biloxi.

After my meeting with Eddie, I stopped by my home to go through some paperwork in my office there. After fifteen minutes or so, my phone rang. It was Carlos. When I heard his voice, I almost jumped out of my skin, eager to hear something about Cecil Campbell, but he surprised me with a message from Isabella. "She called me here in El Paso wanting to know why you haven't called her. She said she has never met a man like you. I think she is in love with you, mi amigo."

"To tell you the truth, Carlos, she has not been far from my mind since I saw her last in Allende. But I have been busier than hell trying to put two and two together with the Gerald Hinson bullshit and helping to run a business and an election campaign here in Mississippi."

"All I can tell you, Delbert, is don't let this woman slip out of your fingers. She is a special senorita."

"Twenty years younger than I am. She wouldn't be after an old man's money, would she, Carlos?"

"I would bet my ass on her. She's the real deal."

"I hope so because I am not looking to get burned again by a gold-digging beauty."

"She would be good for you, my friend. She's one in a million, I guarantee. Give her a call when you get a chance."

"Do me a favor if you can speak with her or her sister. Tell her I want to see her again and see if she still thinks I'm not too old for her."

"I believe that matters more to you than it does to her."

"Do you think she would come to Mississippi if I invited her?"

"If you asked, but she would never ask you to let her come. She's too humble."

"Damn, Carlos, you make her sound like an angel."

"Not quite," he said, "but as close as women come these days."

The vision of her lying beside me, tears on her cheeks, made me want to hold her close and comfort her. I could hear myself saying, "It's all right, honey. I understand." And I recalled how beautiful she was as she drifted off to sleep with me holding her.

~

I CALLED MARGE WILSON TO LET HER KNOW I HAD NOT dropped off the face of the earth. She appeared to be happy about that and upbeat about her prospects for the upcoming election. All the while, in the back of my mind, was always the question of what to do next to help solve Carmen's murder. I knew it might take weeks or months if we left everything to the state and federal investigators. They had all the time in the world. I didn't. I was eager to talk with Shirley Campbell again, but I wanted to hear what Gerald Hinson might have to say before I confronted her.

On Friday morning, I checked in with Colonel Holt and Sydney Saperstein, advising them I was paying attention to my construction business while the state and feds did their things, including arranging for the extradition of Hinson. I got a couple of calls from Elrod concerning the money he needed to spend on fence and barn repairs at the ranch. I advised him to meet with all his boarders and set up payment schedules for current and arrears boarding fees. I was certain existing records had been swept up by state investigators, and Elrod would have no way of knowing about the ranch finances. He would be starting new.

It was almost 10:00 a.m. when Carlos called again. "My friend, I am going back to Mexico City this afternoon. There's nothing more I can do here."

"Has your uncle learned anything more about Gerald Hinson?"

"Only that Mississippi officials will be here today to extradite him. He should be there tomorrow, and he says he isn't talking anymore until he gets back home."

Later that morning, I called Colonel Holt. "Are you hearing anything from your contacts in Jackson?"

"Nothing new," he said, "except Mr. Hinson should be on a plane this afternoon, heading our way."

"You know where they're taking him?"

"They're bringing him to Cumbersome County. I assume he'll be held at the adult detention center."

"You know we still owe a visit to Shirley Campbell, but I sure would like to hear what Hinson has to say before we do that."

"That's a good idea. Maybe Hinson will tell us where to find Mr. Campbell. He seems to have disappeared into thin air."

I chuckled. "Well, you know, Colonel, the air is thinner in Mexico City."

He had a good laugh. "Denver, too, but I don't think Campbell's there. Mexico—maybe. Denver—no."

My thoughts went back to Shirley Campbell. I wondered if Eddie was right, and Logan Vice was the man driving her car. I would like to have had those answers then but knew it would be best if I waited for Hinson. I was also wondering what Stu McCarty might have to say when he finally started talking to someone besides his attorney. I sat down in my favorite chair and turned on the television to catch the afternoon news on TV while I chased theoretical solutions through my mind.

My phone rang. It was Saperstein. "Delbert, you may want to watch the local news at 1 p.m. today. I will be with my client on the steps of the courthouse when he announces his resignation. We couldn't trust the county prosecutor, so I cut a deal for Stu McCarty with the state attorney general. I don't believe Stu has done anything wrong, but I wanted to make certain he wouldn't be prosecuted if he cooperates before a grand jury. I think we have the goods on Sheriff Loudermilk and his son, Josh, Harlan Haynes, and Logan Vice."

"Has Jared Barlow from Southern Construction Supply been interviewed?'

"That will be up to the attorney general. I expect him to convene a grand jury. And I expect some of the accused will flip and testify against the sheriff."

"Yeah, this is when the rats start leaving a sinking ship. Let's see how many run for cover, including the county prosecutor."

"It's going to be fun, Delbert, and way overdue."

"How long has this been in the works?"

"With McCarty, you mean?"

"Yes."

"For over a week. But the attorney general has had his eye on the sheriff's department for months. He's real grateful to Stu McCarty for giving him the ammunition he needs to hang Loudermilk's ass."

"Do you think Loudermilk will be arrested before the election?"

"Probably not, but he doesn't stand a snowball's chance in hell of being elected. I've given this matter some thought. He can't be fired, but maybe he'll have the decency to resign so the county executive can appoint someone until the new sheriff takes office."

"That son of a bitch has no decency. To tell you the truth, Counselor, I'd rather be allowed to punch that fat bastard in the gut than see him go to jail. But at least we'll be rid of him and his crew of misfits."

"Delbert, got to go. You know I've told you more than I should, so keep it between you and me. There'll be plenty of time to discuss it with others after Stu resigns this afternoon."

"Sure thing, Counselor. I'll catch you on the news. And Sid, if Loudermilk is arrested, please see if we can't get him in the same damn dog cage he held me in for three nights. I'd like to be the one to deliver him his dried bologna sandwich."

"Maybe you'll get your wish, Delbert."

I wanted to call Isadore but took Saperstein's caution to heart. The colonel would have to find out about the events himself, and knowing him the way I did, I was sure he would learn about it in time to turn on his TV.

MOMENTS AFTER THE NEWS BRIEFING CONCLUDED, MY phone rang. I knew it was the colonel. "You know something, Delbert, I was kind of proud of ole Stu. God bless him. He looked small and pathetic out of uniform, but by gosh, when he spoke up, he showed he really has guts."

"But I think you'll agree he didn't reveal anything we didn't know or suspect."

"Except the extent of drug dealing, especially involving the sheriff's son and Deputy Vice."

"I expected Cecil Campbell's name to crop up when Stu talked about drug dealing, but it never did."

"It would be interesting to see Stu's written statement,

but that will be part of the grand jury testimony. So the public will never get a look at it until the sheriff goes to trial."

"Colonel, something just crossed my mind. I want you to do me a favor. You can take your night guard off at the ranch and put him guarding Stu's home. That boy has kids, and they don't need to be in danger. You never know what Laudermilk and his underlings will do."

"I suppose it would be best to check this out with Saperstein and let him tell Stu we're going to provide protection."

"Yes, I'll call Sydney and let him know. And I just thought of something else. Stu is going to need an income. Can you take him on temporarily?"

"Temporarily or permanently, doesn't matter to me. I can use him."

"I say temporarily because I intend to ask Marge Wilson to make him a sergeant when she takes office."

"Delbert, I'm pleased to say things are falling into place. All we can do now is to wait for the state to complete its investigation and for the grand jury results."

"We still have to hear from Gerald Hinson and Shirley Campbell. We'll know more about her involvement when he spills his guts."

AFTER DINNER, I SETTLED BACK, WATCHING NETWORK new but always keeping in the back of my mind the idea that Shirley Campbell held the key to much of the mystery surrounding Carmen's death. I finished off an after dinner drink and thought about taking a shower before getting ready for bed. I unfolded a couple of drawings furnished with a bid package I needed to review and laid them across the bed as I prepared to undress. After a few minutes, staring at details I had seen for similar projects a hundred times before, I realized my mind was not about to settle on work projects or allow me to go to sleep. I put my wallet back into my pocket and snapped my .38 revolver holster onto my belt. I couldn't wait any longer to talk with Mrs. Campbell.

It was getting dark as I approached the open gate, which was usually closed across the graveled road leading to the front of the house. My lights illuminated a police car parked at the front steps. I stopped my car, got out, and walked the remaining one hundred feet to the house. I looked up to see Logan Vice coming down the steps toward me.

I feigned a laugh. "Damn, Logan! Fancy meeting you here."

"I might say the same thing to you, Mr. Cantrell. To what do we owe the pleasure of your company this time of evenin'?"

"Oh, I just had a hunch I ought to pay a visit to my friend, Shirley. After all, I've done my best to see that she and her boys have been taken care of. It's good to see you're out here doing the same thing unless, of course, you're here to arrest her."

"Delbert, one of these days, your mouth is goin' to overload your ass."

"Damn, Logan. Looks like I was wrong. I thought you would appreciate my sense of humor. By the way, have you arrested any blondes lately?"

His hand slipped down to touch the holster he carried on

his right hip. He wore his usual arrogant grin. "No, Delbert, I ain't. You murdered any blondes lately?"

As he walked by, we were eyeball to eyeball. I turned to watch him pass by me, making certain my back was never turned to him. He opened the door of his patrol car and stood, looking back at me as if he had a momentous decision to make. My best guess was that he wanted to blow my head away, but he might have a difficult time explaining my disappearance, more so than anyone else who might have crossed him.

I pushed my luck. "Did you see your buddy, Stu, on television this afternoon?"

"That lyin' sumbitch?"

"Yeah, that one, Logan. But I thought you two were asshole buddies."

He slammed his car door shut and unsnapped the strap across his holster. "You just keep your shit up, Cantrell, and I might find a damn good reason to shoot your ass."

It occurred to me that the human debris standing before me in his perfectly pressed uniform would carry out his threat if he had half an excuse. It was time to defuse the situation and do what I intended—speak with Shirley Campbell. "Well, Logan, if you shoot me, you may have to explain it to Colonel Holt or kill him too. He's ten minutes behind me."

He looked down the road then toward me. "You ain't particular 'bout the company you keep are you, Delbert?"

"Sure, I am. That's the reason you and I aren't friends, Logan."

"Fuck you, Cantrell." He got into his patrol car, turned for the gate, and kicked up gravel on his way out. A half dozen or more stones struck my arms and legs. I heard the gravel clinking against the side of my truck as he sped by.

I walked up the steps and rang the doorbell. When no one answered, I knocked. After half a minute, Shirley cracked open the door and peeked out. Only a sliver of her face was visible. "Oh, it's you, Mr. Cantrell. I'm sorry, but I'm not feeling well."

I pushed open the door and stepped inside. "Well enough to entertain Logan Vice? You and I need to talk, lady."

She stepped back. "What do you think I can tell you?"

"A hell of a lot. And Mrs. Campbell, we're through playing games."

Her face drained of expression. She turned pale as she made her way to a sofa and sat down. I think she was resigned to the barrage of questions she knew were coming.

I stood above her. "I want to know where your husband is, and more than that, I want you to explain your connection to Logan Vice and Gerald Hinson."

"I've known Logan for a long time—maybe two years."

"How well have you known him?"

"He's a very close friend. And he's been very helpful since Cecil left."

"I bet he has. How about Gerald Hinson? Has he been helpful?"

"Not especially."

"Why did you try to make me believe he was Cecil?"

"I don't know what you're talking about."

"I'm talking about Emilio Sanchez, the man we tracked all across the southern border, believing he was Cecil."

"Please believe me. I still don't know what you're talking about."

"Emilio Sanchez, the man you were supposed to wire money to in Mexico."

"I've never heard of him. It must have been someone posing as me, something Cecil set up."

"It isn't going to do you any good, Shirley. When I leave here, I'm calling my attorney so he can report everything I know about your involvement to the state attorney general. But I'm not leaving tonight until you tell me where we can find your husband."

"I swear I don't know." She began to wring her hands, and tears ran down her face.

"I'm sorry, Shirley, but I have shielded you as long as I can. I would advise you to turn yourself in before I have to."

"What about my boys? What will happen to them?"

"You should have thought of that before you got involved. But if I can help with the boys, I will."

She stood, coming toward me, her arms outstretched, tears flowing freely down her face. I had the idea she wanted to tell me something she had held inside far too long. But I was not about to comfort her. I stepped back. "Sit down now and tell me the truth."

"I'm sorry," she said. "It's Cecil's fault."

"Sure it is, but you've made things a whole lot worse for you and your boys. You can help make things right by telling me where I can find your husband."

"I don't know where he is, but I know he's dead."

29

A LUCKY MAN

From somewhere and for some reason, I found the compassion to take her into my arms and comfort her. Stroking her hair, I held her face against my chest while her body shook with continuous sobbing. One of the boys opened a bedroom door down the hall. "Mama, are you all right?"

"Yes, son," I said. "Your mama is fine. Close your door, please."

She wiped her eyes with her fingertips and turned to look at her son. "I'm OK, Joey. You and Chris watch your shows. I'll be in there in a few minutes."

She looked up at me. "I have to go to my boys. They'll be needing me."

"Yes, they will."

At that moment, I gave thanks to the man upstairs for my fortunate life and thought of all the good things that had come my way. I am such an imperfect man who has managed to live the kind of life few people can ever experience.

Shirley Campbell was a good woman whose comfortable life had been shattered by events in which she never imagined becoming embroiled. I could have asked her a thousand questions, most of which I instinctively knew the answers to, but I didn't ask.

There was no doubt in my mind she had been drawn to Logan Vice when her husband rejected her for Carmen. And Cecil, like other men before him, including me, was mesmerized by Carmen's beauty and southern charm. I wanted to get my hands on Cecil, not because of his affair with her, but because of his betrayal of my trust. Now, that desire to break his neck was intensified by the shambles in which he had left his family. If Shirley killed him, I could not blame her, but I wanted the details.

"How did Cecil die?"

"Logan." She closed her eyes, gathering strength, I supposed to relive events she most certainly wished had never happened. "He shot him."

"Where?"

"In the face. I didn't see it, but that's what Logan told me."

"No, I mean, where did it happen?"

"Outside on the driveway, down near the gate."

"Do the boys know?"

"They were asleep. I think they still believe their father will be coming home."

"Why did Logan do it?"

"It was my fault," she said. "Logan should never have been here. But I thought Cecil was in Mexico. He came back two nights after I drove him to Slidell." She looked away, avoiding my eyes, probably ashamed of her affair with

Logan. "We were in the bedroom when Cecil came to the front door. He knocked and called my name. I was afraid of what he might do. Logan went to the door with his police revolver. When he came back, he was frantic, said he had something to take care of."

"What happened then?"

"I think Logan made a call to someone. I don't know what they said to each other. Shortly after that, Logan left, and I didn't see him until the next day. Said he took care of everything."

"I asked him what he did with Cecil's body, but he only said he couldn't say, but a guy owed him a lot of favors. He handled it."

"Did you find out what they did with the body?"

"No. I was so confused and conflicted. I had too much to think about. In spite of everything, I loved Cecil. I couldn't bear to know what happened, so I didn't ask."

"Did Cecil kill Carmen?"

"He never admitted it, but I believe he did. He told me he shot John Williams, the guy that burned in your company truck. I think Gerald Hinson was involved, too."

"Why did you help Hinson try to escape to Mexico?"

"I was just doing what Logan told me to do. He said no one would care about GG—he always called him GG—and everyone would think Cecil burned in your truck. He was afraid GG might get arrested for drugs or something else and start talking. So, he wanted him out of the country and said they would never find him in Mexico."

"Was there really someone named Emilio Sanchez?"

"Yes, an illegal that Logan almost arrested several months ago. I don't know if that was his real name, and I never met him. I think he paid Logan to let him go. Logan kept the man's ID card. He said it might come in handy."

"Why did you lead me on a wild goose chase in Mexico looking for Cecil?"

"It was Logan's idea. He hoped your people would stay away from El Paso or San Diego and that everyone would believe Cecil fled to Juarez, Mexico."

It took me a few moments to piece together her convoluted story. I still had my doubts about her version of events, but I had little else to go on.

"You've told me so many lies. Why should I believe you now?"

"Maybe you shouldn't. But I've been so scared and concerned for my boys. I lied, thinking I was protecting them, but I just made things worse. I'm through lying and through trying to protect anyone but my children. I made that decision last night, and my attempts to make things right started this evening with me telling Logan I never wanted to see him again. He's no good. I've known that all along, and I have no excuses for continuing to see him. I was hurt and stupid—but not anymore."

"This is not over for you by a long shot."

"I know I'll probably be arrested."

"I don't think there's any way to avoid it, but more than that, you're in real danger until John Loudermilk is behind bars."

"I deserve whatever comes my way. There's no one to blame but myself. I don't want my boys to suffer over the awful things Cecil and I have done."

"I hope you're telling me the truth, Shirley. If you are, I

know a good lawyer. And you won't have to worry about his fee."

"Why would you help me after all the problems I've caused you and so many others?"

I pointed to the bedroom door down the hall. "Joey and Chris. They're going to need their mother."

Through her tears, she managed to smile as she grasped my hand. "You're a good man, Mr. Cantrell."

"I'm a lucky man," I said.

30

DREDGING UP A KILLER

s soon as I started home, I dialed Colonel Holt. "Colonel, Cecil Campbell is dead, and I think I know who killed him."

"Who, his wife?"

"No, Colonel, her lover, Logan Vice. Seems he has a lot more to answer for than drug dealing and grand theft."

"Where'd you get this?"

"Shirley Campbell. I just left her."

"What makes you think she suddenly began telling the truth, Delbert?"

"I just know. Take it from me, Isadore, I just know."

And I believed I knew with certainty.

That night, for the first time in a long time, sleep came easy. It was not that my troubles were all over, but I believed the truth was slowly ebbing its way out of the murk we were all mired in for the past month. I was confident that Shirley Campbell was finally being honest, and her greatest sin was attempting to protect her children the best way she knew how. As exhausted as I was, I looked forward to the next day when other parts of the puzzle might fall into place. I drifted off with images of a dark-haired Mexican beauty falling gently on my mind.

I awoke the next morning, showered, dressed, and made my way downstairs where Josie was ready to prepare a breakfast of eggs, bacon, and orange juice for me.

"Where's Luis this morning?"

"Working in the yard, why?"

"I would like company for breakfast, so fix enough for the three of us."

While I waited for Josie and Luis to join me at the small table in the breakfast nook, I called Saperstein and filled him in on the events of the previous evening. His skepticism was no less than that of Isadore, but I assured him that Shirley was exhausted, bewildered, and willing to cooperate fully with the authorities.

"Did she tell you anything new?"

"That Cecil Campbell died at the hands of Logan Vice and that Cecil confessed to killing John Williams."

"Did he confess to killing your wife?"

"No, Counselor, but she believes he did. But hell, she's guessing like the rest of us."

Breakfast came, and I told Sydney I would call him again after talking with the colonel. "I'm anxious to know what Gerald Hinson has to say. It might differ from what Shirley Campbell is telling us."

"Wouldn't surprise me, Delbert."

"By the way, I have a new client for you."

"Don't tell me." His remark reminded me just how well Sydney Saperstein knew me.

"Yes, Sid. Shirley Campbell."

"I appreciate the business, Delbert, but you know what they say—a fool and his money are soon parted."

"It's only money, Counselor—just money."

As we ate our meal, we discussed all the things Luis and Josie had taken care of while I played detective and ran off to Mexico. Then I got around to the real reason for inviting them to breakfast with me. "I've been thinking about inviting someone to live with us for a while."

Josie dropped her head and covered her eyes with her napkin. I heard a subdued moan from beneath it. "Not Miss Metzger, I hope, Mr. Delbert. She's cunning."

I touched her hand. "No, no, Josie, not Vicky Metzger."

"Will you still need me to take care of you?"

"Whatever I do, it won't affect you or Luis. Both of you have a place with me as long as you wish."

Luis smiled. "We want you to be happy, Mr. Delbert, that's all." He spoke to Josie in Spanish. "No es true, carino. Not Miss Metzger."

Josie nodded as she pulled the napkins away from her face. She was smiling.

"Don't worry, Josie. It isn't going to happen right away. Besides, I haven't invited her yet. She might refuse."

AROUND NOON, ISADORE CALLED. "DELBERT, I JUST GOT off the phone with Colonel Stanley. His people brought Gerald Hinson in last night. He's at the adult detention center awaiting arraignment on a ton of charges. Seemed he spilled his guts on his way back to Mississippi. Before the day is out, Logan Vice will probably be arrested with more to come after the attorney general convenes a grand jury."

My pulse quickened. It was difficult to comprehend that our quest was coming to an end and that Gerald Hinson, a worthless piece of shit, held the key to resolving Carmen's murder. The last thing on earth I wanted was to owe gratitude to that son of a bitch.

The colonel continued. "You might be interested to know that state police and divers are preparing to drag the river around Escatawpa River Bridge on I-10. They think they'll find Cecil's body there or downriver."

"How about meeting me someplace, Colonel? I want to know everything you've learned."

"How's my office?"

"Yeah, I'll be there in an hour."

"By the way, Delbert, according to Hinson, it was Cecil who murdered John Williams and Carmen. "I'll fill you in with the details when you get here."

"That confirms what Shirley Campbell told me about Williams."

THE COLONEL HAD A POT OF COFFEE FIXED WHEN I arrived. He took a seat behind his desk and motioned for me to sit across from him. He sighed with apparent satisfaction. "Delbert, this has been one difficult slog. And I can't remember when I've enjoyed working with anyone as much as I have with you. I kind of hate to see this thing come to an end, but it looks as if it will soon."

"I don't know what I would have done without you, Colonel."

"Let's see how it turns out. Now, to Gerald Hinson."

"Yeah, to Gerald Hinson."

"Like I told you on the phone, he spilled his guts and put himself right in the middle of the whole mess. I think he wanted as much as anything to hang Logan Vice. Apparently, Hinson didn't care very much for the company he was keeping. I'm sure he'll use that to get himself the best deal possible."

"What did he have to say?"

"Hinson and Campbell had done a few drug deals. They got to know each other while hanging around the ranch. The night Carmen was killed, Hinson was out at Jimbo's Watering Hole—you know the place. It's off Main, around the corner from the co-op."

"Yeah, I know the place—had a beer there once, and once was enough."

The colonel continued. "I was getting ready to say that Campbell called Hinson in a panic—said he just shot Williams for fucking his woman—those are his words—and he needed help disposing of the body. When Hinson got to the ranch, he learned that Carmen was in the tack room where Campbell had left her for dead. Hinson put a bullet in the back of her head 'just to make sure and put her out of her misery,' as he said."

That evoked a vision I cringed at imagining what Carmen must have gone through. I suppose my feelings were evident on my face. The colonel asked. "You OK with this, Delbert?"

"Yes, I need to hear what happened."

"They loaded Williams in his truck, and Hinson drove him to a swamp above Highway 57 with Campbell following in your company truck."

"Did he say why they didn't take Carmen's body, too?"

"That's the odd part. Apparently, Campbell had other ideas, but on the way out with the body of Williams, they met a woman driving into the ranch."

"That would have been Vicky, just as she said."

"Yes. Anyway, they didn't return to the ranch for fear of being seen. Instead, they went back to the Watering Hole and got high."

"I'm puzzled. When did they decide to torch my truck with Williams in it?"

"The next day, Campbell decided he needed to disappear. He must have known he would be a suspect in Carmen's murder. And according to Hinson, Campbell didn't want to face you, especially after you were arrested for his crime."

"And that night, Shirley drove him to Slidell, thinking he was on his way to San Antonio."

"Too bad for him he didn't continue to Mexico. Maybe he wouldn't have ended up in the Escatawpa River." I took some satisfaction from that comment.

LOGAN VICE WAS ARRESTED BY STATE TROOPERS THAT afternoon. No doubt, his bravado notwithstanding, he would sing like a canary. Almost certainly, Sheriff Loudermilk had to understand he would be the next one to be arrested. Gerald Hinson would probably implicate Shirley Campbell as an accomplice in the murder of her husband and the burning of the body of John Williams. How many others would be swept up in the grand jury investigation was anybody's guess.

I planned to do all I could to keep Shirley from going to prison by placing her in the capable hands of Sydney Saperstein, not because of Shirley but because her two boys needed her. There was nothing to do but wait, and that would be damn hard for me and probably the colonel as well.

We had one project to keep both of us busy, and that was to do everything we could to get Marge Wilson elected. With the election only two weeks away, we were optimistic that better days were ahead for the folks of Cumbersome County. The headlines would most certainly not do her opponents any good.

"You know, Delbert, I don't take a lot of satisfaction in the outcome. Too many people have been hurt in the process."

"Me too, Isadore, and it isn't over for me by a long shot. I'll be reliving every damn event through investigations and trials for the next two years. And I still have to arrange for the cremation of Carmen's body. Of course, there'll be a memorial service, but I'll leave the details to her mother and sister."

"You're always doing something for others. When are you going to do something just for yourself, Delbert?"

"You know, Colonel, I'm starting to feel that way too. I'm kind of tired of living by myself."

"Not thinking about getting married again, are you?"

"No, not that, but I do want some female companionship."

"You know, these days, you don't have to marry a woman to get her to live with you. That Vicky Metzger woman looks like a pretty hot number. That wouldn't be bad company."

"She's hot all right, but she's not a woman I want to spend a lot of time with. I have someone else in mind. Maybe she will visit me for a while. It could turn into something much more than that."

"The young senorita from Mexico?"

"Yes, Isabella."

He smiled. "I don't often give advice to the lovelorn, but be careful, old man."

"I will, but I will let you judge for yourself when you meet her."

THE 6 P.M. NEWS WAS INTERRUPTED BY A SPECIAL bulletin, reporting that a body believed to be that of Cecil Campbell, suspected killer of Carmen Cantrell, was found by police divers in the Escatawpa River, lodged behind the bridge pilings. TV cameras, located on the bridge above, beamed down on the recovery efforts below. There was nothing to see except a dark green sleeping bag, in which apparently a body and weights to hold it down were contained.

My thoughts turned to the two Campbell boys. I hoped they were not watching television at that moment. As for Shirley Campbell, perhaps it was altogether fitting that she should see what she might have prevented if she had not helped her husband or become involved with Logan Vice.

Moments later, my phone rang. It was the colonel. "Delbert, are you watching?"

I wasn't ready for any more surprises, and I hoped the colonel had none. "Wouldn't miss it for the world."

"It just occurred to me—what if Cecil Campbell is not the body in the sleeping bag?"

"Why do you ask, Colonel? Do you know something I don't know?"

"No, just one more twist, Delbert."

"I'm through being surprised, not even if we learn Campbell is somewhere in Mexico."

"Living it up on a beach in Cozumel."

I laughed. "Wouldn't that frost your ass, Colonel?"

The colonel laughed, too. "That thought is not too farfetched. You'll never make a good detective, Delbert. You're not suspicious enough."

"You know what I'm going to do, Colonel? I'm going to eat my dinner, then go to bed and sleep like a baby. I suggest you do the same. Cecil Campbell will soon be on a stainless steel table in the morgue with the pathologist carving off his nuts."

"Goodbye, Delbert," the colonel said.

"Goodbye, Isadore."

EPILOGUE

This story might have given you the idea that Cumbersome County is not a nice place to live. But as I write this, the last days of spring are waning, and summer is just around the corner. Here in the county, all along the back roads and even the main highways, farmers have set up their produce stands, offering fresh fruits and vegetables, especially corn, watermelons, and cantaloupes. Folks are friendly and welcoming here. Most attend church and are always willing to lend a hand to their neighbors and, for that matter, strangers. We have to make sure it remains that way. We can do that by electing honest officials who put their constituents ahead of their personal ambitions and greed. The election of Marge Wilson as sheriff was a good start.

Marge was elected sheriff on the first Tuesday in November. She took office on January 1, 2023, but not before Sheriff John Loudermilk and two of his deputies, Harlan Haynes and Stu McCarty, were arrested and charged with receiving bribes and grand theft. Luckily, Stu McCarty is in the capable legal hands of Sydney Saperstein and has turned state's evidence. Hopefully, he will not spend time in prison. Sheriff Loudermilk is also under investigation for abetting drug dealing in our county and his possible involvement in the murder of Cecil Campbell.

Elrod Jones and his wife took a real liking to their life at Oakwood Ranch. Elrod bought two fine quarter horses, and he and his wife are taking riding lessons from Vicky Metzger. I expect to see the Oakwood enterprise become a thriving business—one that I won't have to worry about. But, having learned a hard lesson about trusting people too much, I will not get too far away from it.

Despite Colonel Holt's misgivings, it was Cecil Campbell's body in the sleeping bag dredged up by the state police. Logan Vice is being held at the adult detention center, charged with a myriad of crimes, including the murder of Cecil.

I suppose the most tragic figure in the preceding events is Shirley Campbell. My efforts to minimize her participation and to protect her two sons were to no avail. She was arrested for aiding and abetting and conspiracy to commit murder. I still wish I could keep her out of prison, but I think she is bound to serve several years in the Mississippi State Prison. Saperstein declined to defend her. Now, she is being represented by a court-appointed lawyer. I understand that Shirley's sister and brother-in-law are now living in the Campbell house, taking care of the boys.

Marge Wilson began reforming the sheriff's department immediately after assuming office. She fired two other deputies for questionable conduct. Vacancies created by Elrod Jones leaving, the arrest of Logan Vice, and Marge Wilson's elevation to sheriff left the department with only one deputy. In the short term, she deputized Colonel Holt, who agreed to serve until Marge found qualified applicants. She is keeping her promise to voters to fill vacancies without consideration of sex or race. Such policies might not be to the liking of all the citizens of Cumbersome County, but most people I know appreciate a sheriff who is honest, fair, and keeps her word.

My guest from Mexico arrived one week before Christmas, and she stayed with me until the end of January. The two of us attended Keith's wedding in Dallas, not because I approved, but because I love my brother. I want him to be as happy as I am now that Isabella is in my life. She was still waiting for a ring when I sent her home at the end of that month. Two weeks later, she called to tell me she wanted to return to the States and live with me even if I never married her. She has been here in Mississippi with me since March of this year. We plan to marry before next Christmas. Carlos and Natalia will attend. So will Colonel Holt and Sydney Saperstein.

You know, there was a time when I loved Carmen more than anyone else on this earth. But, like so many other relationships, our marriage went awry. I blamed Carmen, but I suppose we should have shared the blame equally. My work kept me away from home most days until late in the evening. Frequent travel to inspect out of state worksites kept me on the road. Carmen found ways to occupy herself, first with her horses, then with other men. She was too beautiful to stay alone for too long. I could have participated more with her equine interests, but I didn't. So, she found other men who would.

I hope I have made my neglect and shortcomings up to her by helping to solve her murder. So many men were swept up in our efforts to arrest the guilty person. I know that someone in that den of misfits pulled the trigger, but with all the finger-pointing and lies, I am not confident I will ever know which scumbag it was. We may never know with certainty who killed Carmen, but we know killers can't hide forever.

ACKNOWLEDGMENTS

I must acknowledge Frank Eastland and his team at Publish Authority, with special mention to Janie Mills, my editor, and Raeghan Rebstock, my book cover design lead. Their working closely with me as a team throughout this project has been rewarding and is most appreciated. I also wish to thank Tracy Adams, tracyadamscreative.com, for her cover design ideas.

Most of all, I acknowledge my wife, Shirley Adams, whom I love and appreciate for her diligence in working with me on this manuscript until we reached the point where we thought it was right.

ABOUT THE AUTHOR

Travis Short is a successful author who has published several books in various genres. His latest novel, *Anna: A Life of Faith and Courage,* is widely acclaimed. Originally from southwest Virginia, he served in the US Navy before retiring as Lieutenant Commander. Following his military career, he began working in management positions and eventually became a business owner in the shipbuilding and machinery manufacturing industries. After retiring from his second career, he now writes full time. Travis is a proud father of four daughters and three sons and currently resides in Dahlonega, Georgia, and Moss Point, Mississippi, with his wife, collaborator, editor, and love, Shirley Adams.

For more about the author, his books, and his upcoming book events, you are invited to visit his website at TravisShort.com.

THANK YOU FOR READING

If you enjoyed *Killers Can't Hide*, we invite you to leave a review online and share your thoughts and reactions with friends and family.